THE
ENUMERATOR

Agnes Bushell

BIRMINGHAM LIBRARIES
DISCARD

21/4/07

Library of Congress Catalog Card Number: 96–70960

A complete catalogue record for this book can be
obtained from the British Library on request

The right of Agnes Bushell to be identified as the author
of this work has been asserted by her in accordance
with the Copyright, Designs and Patents Act 1988

Copyright © 1997 Agnes Bushell

First published in 1997 by Serpent's Tail,
4 Blackstock Mews, London N4, and
180 Varick Street, 10th floor, New York, NY 10014

Phototypeset in 10 pt ITC Century by
Intype London Ltd
Printed in Great Britain by
Mackays of Chatham plc, Chatham, Kent

For Christopher Monahan

PRELUDE

He got off the elevator and padded down the carpeted hallway to the apartment door. The door was slightly ajar so when he knocked on it, it swung open. He hesitated for a minute, thought about calling out, thought better of it, walked in.

The foyer was brightly lit, done in faux marble with thick white carpeting, its glass table holding an enormous bouquet of irises and exotic lilies, the sweet fragrance of the flowers thick as a presence. He walked across the foyer into the darkened living room where larger, more elaborate floral arrangements gave off their scent and, gallery lit, threw pointed, leafy shadows against the white walls and onto the rug. There was another massive shadow against the wall as well, the shape of a crucifix, the size of a man.

Directly across from it was an open door.

Inside someone was vomiting loudly.

He walked to the door.

The ceiling spot lights were blinding after the darkness of the living room. In the middle of the room, in the center of the lights, surrounded by tall ferns, stood an immense four-poster bed, the foot toward the door. Thick vines climbed up the two back corner posts so that they resembled an arbor. Suspended there between those two vine-covered posts was a black man, naked, tied spread-eagle to the posts by ankles and wrists. His entire head was wrapped mummy-like in green tape. The flesh of his neck, shoulders and chest had been punctured many times, and flowers of all kinds all had been woven into the wounds so that his head resembled a stamen and his torso a bouquet. From a longer, deeper cut below his navel fern-like leaves emerged, but some of his intestines protruded out as well, like the thick, white roots of plants that escape their pots in search of water, or tendrils of vines deprived too long of the sun.

The room smelt overwhelmingly of flowers and decay.

He tried to move, but he couldn't budge. Somewhere to his right someone was still vomiting, and running water in a sink. He got scared then, swallowed hard, found his body could move again, began backing out of the room.

But a man in a t-shirt and jeans appeared at the bath-room door, came across the bedroom toward him, his face ashen, beads of sweat, or maybe it was water, still on his forehead, his lips, dripping from his chin. He kept backing away, but the man caught him in the doorway, gripped him by the shoulders, his fingers sinking into his flesh like teeth.

What do we do now? he said, over and over. *What do we do now?*

That's how it all started.

More or less.

CHAPTER 1

The enumerator came knocking on our door one night while we were discussing the nature of the soul.

It was a Wednesday in mid-January, the year the drought ended, that wonderful winter of tremendous rains. Everything was green, moist, lush. People had begun washing their cars in public again, flushing their toilets after every use. Water was pouring down on us out of the skies; we felt redeemed, blessed. I don't know how the rest of the city reacted, but in my household this feeling of redemption and blessing led inevitably to long after-dinner conversations on the existence of the soul.

So we were smoking pot, drinking beer, and comparing the Hindu and Taoist ideas of soul with the Christian version, just your typical Wednesday night at home, when the enumerator knocked on the door. It was only then that Evan remembered he had made an appointment with this guy to be interviewed for an AIDS study the University was doing. Interviewers were going around different neighborhoods—our neighborhood, the Castro, gay capital of the world, was, of course, one of them—visiting every eighth household, enumerating the men who lived there, and if they were the right age, interviewing them about their sexual practices. Evan would get ten bucks for participating and the satisfaction of knowing he had done his civic duty as a San Franciscan during the plague years. But he wasn't quite sure he was up to discussing his sex life at the moment. He was having too much fun talking about God to get bummed out over sex.

"Poor, poor Evan," I said, and opened the door.

Just one look at the enumerator and I thought, Oh my God, any day I'd talk to him about *my* sex life.

Like he'd be interested.

His name was Sean.

He was gorgeous.

He was gay.

"Evan's not home," I sighed, gazing into the dark, sultry eyes of Sean the Enumerator. "He's out getting laid so he'll have something to tell you about when you come back."

Evan called out from the living room, "Oh, let him in, Alexandra. I won't tell him about how you seduced me when I was thirteen, I promise."

"Excuse me," I said, "but that's not how it happened. *He* seduced *me*." I said to the beautiful stranger at the door. "He's always been out of control. I used to change his diapers, I know. Welcome to the House of Incest."

Sean just smiled at me. His smile was gentle and patient, as though he had heard everything and forgiven everyone. He seemed in general to have a high tolerance for pain of all kinds. His left eyebrow was pierced and he had a thick geometric tattoo that looked Druidic or Celtic around his left arm. His whole body was probably pierced and tattooed. Once you start on that road, it's hard to stop. Believe me. I know.

Sean sat down on the floor with us. He looked like a regular person so it was hard to take him seriously as a sex surveyor. That's what people say about narcs, too: they seem just like regular people until they bust you.

We were hospitable. We offered him drugs, alcohol, cigarettes, ice cream, a latte if he were really insistent. But he declined everything and said he really probably ought to make another appointment. A good take on the scene, I thought, though Evan kept saying it was no problem, but of course at that point Evan's soul had become so Hindu and universal he would probably have given the sexual history of every one of his fifty-nine past lives. Jake came to the rescue. He was also in the survey, and since he was cold sober as always (preserving his mental acuity along with his vital fluids for his T'ai Chi exercises), he would be happy to switch appointment times with Evan. Fine. So he and Sean slipped away into the kitchen for privacy and Evan and I resumed our conversation, now for some reason centering on the relationship between souls and sex, if any.

Twenty minutes later, Jake and Sean emerged from the kitchen, shook hands, parted amiably. Very nice, professional, I thought.

"That didn't take too long," Evan said. "I thought it would take longer. Or didn't you have that much to say?"

Jake got himself a Red Tail from the refrigerator and sprawled out on the sofa. We waited for him to say something, but he didn't.

"Well?" I said finally.

"Well what?"

"Well, how was it?"

"Not bad," he said. And then he said, "It's kind of a bummer, though. Makes you think about all the sex you're not having."

"Don't look at me," I said.

"Me either," said my brother, the Hindu with a Sense of Humor.

"It's a lousy time to be gay," Jake said. "I mean, I'm very sympathetic and all. But, shit, it's an even lousier time to be straight."

Men, I thought. How they love to universalize!

I spent the next day looking for a job, which is what I'd been doing for the five weeks I'd been in San Francisco. There were no jobs, or at least no jobs I wanted to do. I wasn't desperate enough yet to go after the café jobs. I was still hoping to find something in photography, dark-room work, printing.

I'd just come back to California from New Mexico. I'd been working in a Bed and Breakfast in Taos and taking photographs all over the Southwest. I was into rocks, petroglyphs, the textures of the earth. By the time I left, I had friends among the Indians at Taos Pueblo and was making photographs of people's faces there that all wound up having the texture of rock and petroglyph and the earth. I fell in love in Taos, but it didn't work out.

Yes, I had a slightly bruised heart, not that it stopped me from rejoicing that I was back in San Francisco. Even jobless, aimless and without a boyfriend. I had my camera, I had another paycheck coming, and when all else failed—as it probably would—I had my brother, a good Capricorn, always employed, who wouldn't let me sleep on the streets no matter how often I embarrassed him in the presence of strangers.

I didn't find a job that day, not unexpectedly as I spent most of the afternoon in a little tattoo parlor on Columbus choosing a tattoo to mark this passage into a new state of being.

"I'm thinking of putting it on my left bicep," I said that evening, tossing the design onto the kitchen table for all to see. "Like wearing your heart on your sleeve. What do you think?"

Evan glanced at the image of the heart surrounded by thorns and flames.

"Like wearing Jesus' heart on your sleeve you mean. What is this, Zand, a return to the icons of your childhood or something? This reminds me of the funeral parlor calendar Grandma had hanging in her kitchen."

"I think I deserve the Sacred Heart. I've suffered," I said.

"Please," he said. "Spare me."

"He was the love of my life."

"He was a jerk."

"You never met him."

"I met the other ones. The head-banger, the punk poet, the Nigerian prince—what a winner he was. The tough with the Harley and 'Choose Death' painted on his helmet. The artist with attitude. The junkie who ripped off your apartment. The . . . "

"OK, fine. Eat me, OK?"

I took my Sacred Heart of Jesus and stuffed it in my back pocket. Left bicep, I thought. That's the spot. Evan meanwhile had gone back to reading the paper, Jake to his stir fry. Tonight's dinner, something with vegetables and tofu. When it was my turn I intended to blast them through the roof with Taos chili. Get that old blood moving in their stodgy old veins.

"Let's go the movies or something," I said.

"Can't. Sean's coming over. AIDS study night. Clean and sober. Confession time."

"Well, after. How long will it take? I mean, unless you want to borrow some of *my* sexual history, which you seem so very familiar with . . ."

"Sean said the straight interviews only take twenty minutes no matter how much history you have," Jake said, a wee bit defensively, I thought. "We are basically not of much interest . . ."

"Tut, tut," I said. "For once the straight white male is basically not of much interest . . ."

"Notice, however, that they don't bother with women at all."

"I noticed," I said. "That's because we don't get AIDS. We are merely conduits. We just pass it along to men. Women who claim to be positive are just hysterical. They're attention seekers. And women who die of AIDS . . . well, it's like hysterical pregnancy, you know? It's hysterical pneumocystis . . ."

"Alexandra," my brother said, "shut up."

Sean arrived right on time, 8 o'clock sharp. He was wearing black again. Again he was totally adorable. Black clothes, black hair, gold rings in his ears, one in his eyebrow, that gorgeous Celtic tattoo around his arm. But Sean was not his gentle, amiable, cooled out, laid-back self tonight. He was slightly hyper, slightly out of control. So I asked. If he was OK. If anything had happened. If I should call the Gay Guardian Angels or something.

"No. No, I'm fine, thanks," he said. But he was lying.

I said, "You know, you don't lie very well."

"I don't?" he said. "I always thought I did." And he smiled at me the way gay men don't generally smile at me. Like he was really seeing me. Like he was *looking*.

"If this were a '30s movie I'd offer you a shot of whiskey or something," I said. "We have a little scotch. But you're working, right, so I shouldn't tempt you."

"I could be tempted," he said, and again I felt that sexual energy floating across the room at me and I thought, Whew, I must be imagining things. I must be so horny I'm just making all this up.

"Do you mind if I sit down?" he asked.

"Please," I said, offering him a chair at the table. He sat down heavily, like someone who'd been on his feet all day. The *Chronicle* was still lying there on the table, folded over to an article on page 6. He glanced at it and then looked up at me. I was surprised by the expression on his face, or maybe it was the lack of expression, as though he were too exhausted to react to anything.

"Did you read about this?" he asked. "The man who was murdered in his condo by Buena Vista Park?"

I hadn't. I rarely read the newspaper anymore. But this was a particularly grisly murder, so of course Jake had read the story out to us over dinner.

"The florist?" I asked, choosing the least gory of the details I remembered. He had been beaten and stabbed to death.

"Yeah," he said. "The florist. Lamont Bliss."

He sounded so depressed, I just took a gamble. "Did you know him?"

"No. But I'm enumerating in that building. I was in that building Tuesday night. The night he was killed. The same night. I can't believe it."

"Jesus," I said. "Want that scotch?"

"No, I can't. But thanks. Is your brother home?"

"Yeah," I said. "He's just in there making himself beautiful for you." And then I added, quickly. "Just kidding." I didn't want him to get his hopes up.

"I just can't believe it," he said again, like he hadn't heard anything I'd said. "Lamont Bliss."

"Was he going to be in the study?" I asked him. Lamont had been identified in the paper as "a well-known figure in the Castro whose work on the Gay Pride Day floats made him the most popular floral designer in the gay community." Or something along those lines.

"No. He was too old."

"How old is too old?"

"Over thirty. He was thirty-five."

"And you were there?"

"Well, I was in the building. I mean, so were a lot of people. It's a huge building, the old children's hospital, that pink palace on the top of the hill? You must know the one."

Of course I knew it. You could see it sitting up there above Buena Vista Park from practically all over the city.

"And he was killed after midnight, they say. I wasn't there then. It's still creepy."

"They didn't discover the body until the next night. Somebody made a phone call. That's pretty creepy too."

"He didn't show up at work. Why didn't they check it out then?"

I didn't know. I didn't know why Sean was so hung up on this either. But he was.

"His shop is right around here," I said, scanning the article on the page in front of me. "Mount Bliss Flowers. On 18th Street."

"Keep reading," he said. "The part about bringing home white skinheads from lower Haight. The S and M stuff. Seems his friends knew all about it. Think they might have tried a little intervention."

"This town's too tolerant for intervention," I said.

"This town's full of fucking zombies," Sean said. "They're not tolerant. They're too self-absorbed to be tolerant. They're just oblivious. Soul-dead. You could drop off the planet in front of them and they wouldn't even notice. People do, too. All the time."

"You're not from here," I said, gambling on my powers of deduction. "You'll get used to it."

At this point my brother swept into the room from the john smelling of Zino (The Fragrance of Desire) and wearing his Straight But Not Narrow t-shirt.

Nothing like sending mixed signals, Evan.

The interview went as quickly as Jake's had. Evidently there was no closet in my brother's life that part of him was hiding in, the part that might have dressed well and had a decent sense of humor.

CHAPTER 2

My feelings of compassion for men traumatized by a casual encounter with victims of urban crime usually last about five seconds, so by the time Sean left I was over it and ready to be entertained. Hey, it's Thursday night, guys. Let's start warming up for the weekend.

But Thursday night is *Star Trek* marathon night: a *Next Generation* re-run at 7, *Deep Space* at 8, a new *Next Generation* at 9. It's a perfect modernist fantasy, *Star Trek*, in which the Good, in the form of friendship, loyalty, reason and honor, always emerges victorious. It must be a fantasy we postmodernists yearn for with incredible nostalgia because all over the city, people of all ages spend Thursday evenings glued to their TVs with the idea that at 10 they'll venture out for that beer . . . but by 10 they're so brain dead they can't find the front door.

We'd missed the full triple bill thanks to Sean, but he was barely out the door before Evan switched on the tube for the last half-hour of *Deep Space 9* and Jake started passing around the Red Tails. Incorrigible, I thought. No wonder they never get laid. But then I got hooked, too, cozied down on the couch with them to drink Red Tail and veg out.

I have to admit that I love my brother and cozying down with him to watch *Star Trek* spin-offs is actually close to my idea of paradise. Add a six-pack of Red Tail and it *is* paradise.

Evan wanted to be a priest at one time in his life. Then he wanted to be a doctor. Then he wanted to be on one of those rock-climbing rescue teams that save people stranded on top of mountains in blizzards. Now he putts around the Bay monitoring water pollution levels and going after toxic waste dumpers with the wrath of God and a bunch of city, state and federal prosecutors in tow. Salvation in one form or another. He also works at an AIDS hospice because he still wants to be a priest/doctor/rescuer of stranded men on mountaintops, plus he actually likes dying people. He says they're a thousand times nicer than anybody else and he's always learning about how to be a human being from them. How to die, I guess, is what he's learning.

They go to a better place, he says.

"I hope Lamont Bliss went to a better place," I said as the Enterprise crew smiled knowingly at each other after another successful battle against Evil in the form of interspecies ignorance and the credits came on. "That's Sean's florist. I told you, remember?"

"*Sean's* florist?" he said. "His shop is right around the corner, Zand. He's *our* florist. We all know him. We all buy flowers there."

"Well, chill, OK? We all who?"

"Everybody, the whole neighborhood. Everybody knew Lamont. He flirted with everyone. He flirted with me even."

"Not very discriminating, was he?"

"Can't you stop being sarcastic for one minute?" Sometimes St. Evan loses patience with me. "You're hopeless, you know?" he said. "You have no feelings."

"I have feelings. I just don't dump them all over the place. Why are you being so random?"

"Maybe Sean talked to him once, OK? I talked to him practically every day for the past five years. So did everybody else on this block. He was very well liked. By everybody. Some asshole killed him. I hope they find the motherfucker and I hope they fry him for it."

"Evan? Is that you talking?"

"No," he said. "It's my evil twin."

The phone woke me from an impenetrably dark sleep. It was 11:30. A.M. or P.M., I wondered. Had to be A.M. But, no, it wasn't. It was dark outside, too. It was night.

"Hey, I'm sorry to be calling so late. This is Sean."

"Oh. Sean," I said, thinking hard. "Not the enumerator?"

"Right. That one. I think I left my cases at your house. They were in a kind of leather zipper thing. I'm sorry. But could you look, because if they're not there I'm history, you know?"

The leather zipper thing was on the floor under the kitchen table. I brought it into my room with me and told him it was safe and sound.

He was suitably grateful and asked if he could come and get it first thing in the morning. I said it depended on what his idea of first thing was.

We made a date for ten. He'd bring the cappuccinos and the muffins and the cigarettes. And I thought, Right. And I'll provide the condoms.

Oh, dream on, honey. Dream on.

Sometimes I hate this town.

I was in such a pissed-off mood all of a sudden ("See you tomorrow, Sean." "See you tomorrow . . . Sorry, I don't even know your name . . .") that I unzipped the leather thing and took a handful of folders into bed with me. Bedtime reading, I thought. Secrets of the confessional. Unnatural sexual practices of our times. The raw and the cooked, the uncut and the cut. Tattoo and taboo.

The yellow folders were just for enumerations. This is what Sean must have filled out on us the first time he came by, though I missed him that time. Names, ages and marital status of all the men in the household and then the women and children, should they exist. Along with the yellow enumeration folders were the listing sheets, all the addresses on every block in each neighborhood he visited. Every eighth house or apartment was circled. I guess he'd go up and down the block, stopping at these designated addresses, and then, depending on the enumeration information he got from someone in the house, he'd set up appointments for the interview. That's how it worked with us. He came by on a Thursday night and caught Evan and Jake, two unmarried men under the age of thirty, cuddled up on the couch in *Star Trek* heaven. Bonanza.

The yellow folders were boring. The real juicy stuff was in the white interview folders, CONFIDENTIAL stamped all over them. It gave me chills just to think how sinful I was being, willfully invading someone's privacy, ripping the veil away from the intimate secrets men shared only with each other.

I pulled my quilt up a little closer around my bod, and started to read.

By the time I shut off the light at 3, I was reeling. I must have dreamt about sex, too, because I woke up . . . Well, this isn't about *my* sex life is it, or lack thereof. Anyway, I woke up excited, shall we say, and not because Sean the Untouchable was bringing over cappuccinos for breakfast.

The soul needs to love. It blossoms when it loves. The soul needs passion. Even unrequited love, the melancholy of unrequited love, the heartache, the anguish, the yearning, the longing, even that is good for the soul. It takes us out of ourselves. It makes us better human beings. Suffering is good for us. Isn't that odd? Yes, darling. Queer, but true.

So maybe I would fall in love with queer Sean just to suffer a little and nourish my soul.

I got up even though it was the ungodly hour of 8:15, and stumbled into the kitchen in search of the morning paper. Craziness of this kind means it's time to get serious about a job.

Evan had left the paper open and scrawled a note over page A15. He'd circled a small article on the lower right and written in big letters in black crayon. CAN THIS BE OUR ENUMERATOR? The article reported that a couple walking home around midnight had discovered a body at the foot of the stairs at Noe and Liberty, a white male in his twenties carrying identification as an enumerator for the University's AIDS study. Robbery did not appear to be the motive, since the victim's wallet was still in his pocket. The police had not released the cause of death, and the name of the victim was being withheld pending notification of next of kin.

It couldn't be Sean, who was about to arrive at my door bearing gifts.

He was having breakfast with me in less than two hours, how could he be dead?

I began to feel like I was teetering on a very narrow ledge very high up the side of a mountain.

I began to feel like I couldn't breathe.

Sean, I said. This is crazy. I just talked to you last night. You were here in my house! *Here*, I said. And then I sat down hard on a kitchen chair. It can't be you, I said.

This had all happened already. I was repeating everything he'd said, everything he'd felt. I'd become his

emotion. Denial. Then I became my own emotion: right-
eous indignation. Anger.

I'm comfortable angry. It's because I was born under
the sign of Mars, or because my soul is one of those
hungry ghosts who crave blood. I get Shiva before I get
Jesus, if that makes any sense. I get Jehovah; Buddha
escapes me.

I called the survey center, but all I got was an
answering machine. I didn't have Sean's home number; I
didn't even know his last name. I called Evan at work,
but he was out inspecting somewhere. But while I was
furiously dialing numbers I began to get rational again.
Jesus, Alexandra, I said to myself, there's no reason to
think this dead enumerator is Sean. There are a bunch
of them, after all, and Sean was safe at home at 11:30
P.M., calling me.

Unless he hadn't been home.

What made me think he was home? He could have
been at a public phone, he could have been at someone's
house. He could have been visiting someone up on
Liberty Street . . .

And fallen down the stairs on his way home?

I made myself some coffee and told myself to wait
until 10 to see if someone knocked on my door before . . .
Before what?

I cleared the table and pulled all of Sean's folders and
interviews out of his case. Went through the listing
sheets, and, yes, he had enumerated on Liberty. He had
that whole neighborhood above Dolores Park: Church,
Sanchez, Noe, Castro.

I wasn't sure what I was looking for. Since I couldn't
believe Sean was the enumerator who was found dead
at the bottom of the Liberty Street stairs, I wasn't really
trying to find out who he might have been visiting up
there at 11:30 on a Thursday night, but just in case . . .

I separated the yellow folders into piles by neighborhood. He had about forty of them. I put the interviews aside since I'd already read them and they didn't include the respondents' addresses anyway, only their ID numbers.

Addresses was about all they didn't include, however.

The interview wasn't just a bunch of questions and answers. The interview was a kind of record of the entire conversation, or the respondent's half of it, anyway. The enumerator wrote everything down, not just the "yes"/"no" responses, but all the elaborations the respondent added to the answer. Sean had a very precise hand and he had written down, it seemed almost word for word, everything the man he was interviewing said to him. Everything.

One interview, for example, breaks off when the interviewee or respondent (R. in enumerator shorthand), having described in detail how he fisted his boyfriend, said, "And even talking about it to you . . . You know, I'd like to fuck you the same way, Sean . . ."

In another color ink Sean had written: Interview terminated. No follow-up rescheduled.

I'd read through these. I knew there was a lot in them. A lot. A few of the respondents were romantics—you could hear it when they described their relationships—but most seemed to be just putting notches on their bedposts. Dealing in hyperbole, if you asked me. Straight men and gay men—you can't believe any of them for shit.

I had filled the kitchen table with piles of yellow folders and other piles of white interviews. I was getting ready for bad news by keeping busy. I'd be washing floors soon.

When he knocked on the door and then walked right

in, I was already so resigned to his death that for a split-second I thought that I was seeing his ghost.

I hugged him, but he held me too close and too long and I felt his body respond in a very strange way.

"You're not dead," I said. "I'm so glad."

He kissed me.

"You're not dead," I said again, when I could catch my breath. "And you're not gay."

"No," he said. "Surprise."

CHAPTER 3

Souls might need lust, passion, desire, but they also need comfort and friendship, and despite what his body might be telling both of us, what Sean's soul needed at that moment was a kitchen table, a cappuccino, and a hand to hold, mine to be precise. He needed to talk, too, and I was more than willing to listen.

He'd had what you'd call a rough night.

He'd left our house for his next appointment and was half-way there—and already late—before he realized he'd left his cases behind. Fortunately he didn't need them for this interview; he had blank interviews in his car, and all the paraphernalia he needed to do blood work, which he hadn't bothered to bring to our place since he knew Evan was straight . . .

"How'd you know that?" I asked him, always amazed that men figure these things out so easily, whereas I . . .

"He told me when I was doing the enumeration. Straight men usually do. You know, they're like, Well, I wouldn't mind being in the study, but I'm not gay . . .

Then I jump them with, Cool. 'Cause, see, you don't need to be gay to be in the study. So, you got a few minutes now? . . . They're so predictable, it's almost a form of entrapment."

So he'd gone to his next appointment, which was up on Liberty Street, but the respondent wasn't home. He hung around for awhile, thinking maybe the guy was just late. He was sitting in his car waiting when he saw Jeff Taylor walking down the block.

"It was incredible. I'd never met another enumerator on the street like that. Not ever. So I jumped out of my car and . . ."

He stopped dead, mid-sentence. I waited, but he didn't continue. It was like he was in a trance or something.

"Sean?" I said.

"Maybe I was the last person to see him alive," he said, and I thought I was hearing a little craziness in his voice right then.

"Jeff's the one who . . ."

"Yes."

"Are you sure?"

"I'm sure. I called our supervisor this morning. She told me."

He pulled up his t-shirt. "See this?" he said. Over his heart he had a tattoo of a skull with a snake coming out through one of the eye sockets. "I got this right after I started this job. I wanted death written all over my body . . . Like why not, it's everywhere else, right? I hear about people dying every day. The other day I was talking to this middle-aged man, forty-four, very sick himself. So I have to ask how many men in the household are under forty. That's the first question. He says, My lover was thirty-six, but he's not here now. He's in heaven. He's waiting for me in heaven . . . It pisses me off, to have to ask questions, to have no *answer*. Now, man, I feel like I'm just this death energy, I just *attract* it . . ."

"Sean," I said. "Get a grip. You want a joint or something?"

He didn't.

"So you were telling me about meeting Jeff . . ."

"Yeah. So I saw him walking down Liberty toward Church. We'd been through training together, a real bonding experience, and he was glad to see me, too. He'd also just been deeked by a respondent and had an hour to kill, so we decided to give ourselves a break and go get a coffee.

"Now we're not supposed to discuss cases with each other. That's totally forbidden, but Jeff was really upset about something and so I told him to tell me, that I wouldn't rat him out or anything, that I'd had some weird experiences too, and that we'd just burn out and go nuts if we didn't talk to each other. I mean, we needed an Enumerator Support Group, if you asked me . . .

"He started talking about Lamont, the florist, remember? Jeff knew Lamont. In fact, Jeff was the enumerator originally assigned to that building on Buena Vista Park, but once he discovered that Lamont's apartment was a designated household he told the supervisor he couldn't do the rest of the building and so I got it. We're not supposed to interview people we know, for obvious reasons. And I think Jeff had been involved with Lamont at one time. So even though Lamont was too old for the study, Jeff didn't want to have to interview whoever he was currently dating, whoever was living with him. It could get sticky.

"Then he started telling me this very strange story about a respondent he had interviewed who had second thoughts about it. He called Jeff and told him he had to have the interview back. Jeff said he couldn't do that, but the guy was really upset, like nuts almost, so Jeff said that they could get together and go over it and he would cross out things . . . though he wasn't sure he could do that. And he was in this awkward position of wanting to help the guy, who he said seemed totally paranoid and scared and freaked out about something he had told him, but on the other hand not wanting to get in trouble with the supervisor or lose his job, something they are always threatening us with . . . He didn't even want to ask Lydia if it was OK to cross things out after the interview was over, because he was afraid she'd say no and then start harassing him about it. We're really in this terrible position, you know, caught between the respondents and the supervisors. Like one day I went from an interview with some crazed sex fiend who wanted to fuck me on his kitchen floor to a review with my totally intimidating supervisor who wanted me to clean up my handwriting or she'd fire me. I wanted to say, I'd like to see you try writing neatly while some guy's rubbing your thigh . . . Or telling you he's positive and fucking his boyfriends without wearing a condom and has no intention of changing his behavior, what the hell for, and so you're writing this down, *neatly*, while resisting the urge to stem the epidemic by cutting the asshole's dick off with the garden shears on his windowsill.

"Anyway, Jeff was really struggling with the ethics of all this, like we're supposed to be moral philosophers or something to do this damn job for $9.35 an hour . . .

"At about 10:30 I dropped him back at his car and checked on my respondent, who still was out. Then I found a pay phone and called you."

"You called me at 11:30," I said.

"Well, whatever."

"It was late."

"I know. I'm sorry."

"Do you know what happened to Jeff exactly?"

"He was mugged. Probably right at the top of Liberty Street, and then pushed down the stairs . . . You know, I think you might have saved my life," he said.

"Me? How?"

"Think of it. If I'd had my cases with me, I might have kept enumerating in that neighborhood and it might have been me who got mugged and pushed down the stairs. But I didn't have them because I left them here. And I left them here because on some subconscious level I wanted to leave them here so I'd have an excuse to see you again . . . We're not supposed to date respondents."

"I'm not a respondent," I said. "Wrong gender."

"I know, but that's a technicality. I met you enumerating. You're related to a respondent. I mean, it verges on the unethical."

"But we're not dating."

"Not yet," he said, and he smiled at me and my heart dissolved into little pools of quicksilver. But I was in my practical mode, so I asked him wasn't 10:30 sort of late to be knocking on doors.

"You'd be surprised how many people who are never home ordinarily will answer their doors at 10:30 at night, Thursday nights, especially. It's bizarre."

No it isn't, I thought. You're just hitting the Trekkies.

Then he said, "I remember when I first started this job. I thought it would be interesting, challenging, you know. I thought it would even be fun. Fun! I know so much now, I don't even think about having sex. You say sex to me, I think KS lesions, I think thrush, dementia, brain tumors, pneumocystis, bed sores . . ."

None of this boded too well for my getting laid this morning. I wondered if anyone but homicidal maniacs and incipient suicides were having sex in San Francisco anymore.

"Well," I said, gesturing to the table, "your cases are all right here."

"You were organizing them for me."

"I'm compulsive."

"Really, what were you doing?"

"Trying to figure out if you were coming for breakfast or not."

"Fuck," he said, "I forgot the muffins!"

"Never mind. I'll make us omelettes . . . It was a weird mugging, don't you think? They didn't take anything."

"They didn't?"

"Well, they didn't take his wallet."

"Was it a bashing then?"

"I don't know," I said, thinking of all the sidewalks I've walked on in my own neighborhood that are stenciled by Act Up or Queer Nation with the chilling notice A QUEER WAS BASHED HERE.

"You really thought it was me, huh?"

"You're the only enumerator I know."

"I'm sorry if it upset you."

"It could have been worse," I said. "You like cheese in your omelettes?"

"I think Jeff was scared," he said. "Or he had a premonition . . ."

I didn't want to hear this. I buried my head in the refrigerator looking for the cheese. When I emerged Sean was paging through one of his interviews.

"Did you read these?"

"No, of course not," I said, lying stoutly. "It says confidential in bold letters right on page one."

He nodded and then gathered them up and put them into the leather case.

"I better call Lydia back," he said. "I have a review scheduled for this afternoon. I wonder if she'll cancel. Probably not."

"If she does, want to go to the Park or something?"

"Sure," he said, without too much enthusiasm.

I grated cheese and mixed eggs, got the butter sizzling in the pan. The soul needs food too. Caring for a soul is very much like caring for a body when you come right down to it. Feed it, keep it warm, shelter it from the elements, love it . . .

"Want to put on some music?" I asked him, nodding in the direction of the CDs.

I wondered what state his soul was in. Maybe I could tell from the music he picked out.

I was just swishing the omelette around in the pan when sound entered the room.

Pantera. "Cemetery Gates." Harmonic screams and raging power chords, dark, heavy and very loud.

And you were expecting sex this morning, Alexandra?

CHAPTER 4

The bar of the St. Francis Hotel was pretty empty for a Friday afternoon, though granted it was early afternoon and raining. I'm fond of this bar. It reminds me of my parents, because they'd bring Evan and me here when we were kids, especially around Christmas time so we could ride the cable cars and look at the Christmas lights and the big Christmas tree in Union Square. I like how woody it is, how comfortable, in a formal, adult sort of way, how pleasant the waiters are, how you never know who may drop in for a brandy. I saw Leonard Bernstein here once when I was little. Just for an example.

Actually I'm fonder of the bar than of the person I

was meeting in it. Elizabeth, named, I regret to say, after the Queen of England, on whose coronation day she was born. Oh, what luck! And she's acted like the Queen of England ever since someone was dumb enough to mention it to her.

She was already enthroned at a corner table when I arrived. Late as always. Following the script.

And as always she was well coiffed and well dressed and had parcels and shopping bags (from those chic joints evil Evan and I renamed Wilkes-Bashful, Magnin P.I., Grumps, and, of course, Needless Mark-up) all gathered around her like a bulwark against invasion, or intimacy. We look our parts; Elizabeth could never be mistaken for anything but a Marin matron on a shopping spree. Friday afternoon in town. Drop three or four hundred. Tra la. As for me . . .

I smiled serenely and said, "Did you order for me? A Laphroaig with a splash, no ice."

"Alexandra," she said regally, "you are a sight! My God! How did they even let you in here?"

I glanced at myself in the mirror behind her. I looked like I always do, except that I had actually put a skirt on over my leggings for this little jaunt downtown.

My hair is bottle-blonde, on the platinum side of bleached. It's shaved around my scalp, but longish on top. I like the way it feels, like having bangs all around my head. I have six earrings in each ear, a combination of studs and rings, but no other piercings, not like Sean's eyebrow, or all those pierced noses and lips and tongues you see around. I'm a bit squeamish about holes. Tattoos on the other hand . . . I have five of them, three that could be seen on that particular day: a lascivious bright green snake around my right ankle, a red rose on my right hand, just below the thumb, and a black spider web that was actually on my left shoulder but crept up a bit along my neck. I needed that bleeding heart of Jesus on my left arm if only for aesthetic balance.

Since my tattoos are so colorful, I wear black most of the time. In winter, black leggings, a leather jacket over a black t-shirt, a black leather skirt, hiking boots. I was wearing Ravishing Red lipstick and a little blush, just so I wouldn't look too vampirish for Queen Liz. I thought I looked OK, but I guess you can't satisfy everybody. The St. Francis doorman seemed happy to see me, but my sister's a hard nut to crack.

"You look devastating too, Elizabeth," I said as demurely as possible. "How was shopping? Did you buy any more of those little throw pillows at two hundred bucks a crack?"

"Let's not fight," she said. "I enjoy my life and you enjoy yours. Let's agree to respect the different choices we've made and just have a pleasant drink together for once."

The waiter appeared, I ordered my scotch with a splash, he withdrew.

It's a masculine place, the St. Francis. It tends to mitigate against female hysteria. You don't want to raise your voice here, become shrill. Something about the men's club decor. I like that about it, too.

I let Elizabeth tell me about her life and how she enjoys it. She married a very wealthy man and so she has everything you could want, in triplicate. I adore listening to her talk about how hard it is to get good help. Is it possible for a person to mouth such clichés and not even know it? Or is getting good help really one of the crosses the rich are forced to bear? Is it the sort of suffering that's good for their souls?

I swallowed my shot with a splash and wished for a non-filtered cigarette. Elizabeth was talking about the ballet, the opera season, the Black and White Ball. Meanwhile the bar was filling up a bit. Couples came in shaking wet umbrellas, an unusual and welcomed sight in San Francisco. Someone passed behind my chair and all of a sudden I got a whiff of wet rubber, wet wool, pipe tobacco, ancient odors, and I completely lost what Elizabeth was saying, whatever trivia she was talking about.

It's ridiculous, but every time I come here something reminds me of my father.

"How's Evan?" she was asking. "I haven't even talked to him since Christmas."

"He's fine," I said, trying to focus on her and not see my father's ghost hovering around the table waiting for his Laphroaig libation.

"I worry so much about him. My only brother. I just worry all the time."

"You do? Why?"

"Well, he's still volunteering at that AIDS place, isn't he? I keep asking him to stop. He won't listen, of course, but I worry that he may be exposing himself to that virus. You never know how careful they are, and there's all that blood and everything. I really don't want him to have anything to do with those people, but of course, he never pays any attention."

"I'm sure he's careful, Elizabeth. I think it's important . . ."

"Of course it's important that somebody does it. But why does it have to be Evan? I mean, he's not even gay, for heaven's sakes."

I was tempted to tell her he was just to freak her out, but I didn't. I could tell her I was, but she doesn't adore me the way she adores him, so it wouldn't have the same effect.

I actually stopped to wonder what effect that would

be, exactly. If Evan were gay, would he suddenly be a different Evan to her than he was now?

We puzzle about these things to no satisfactory conclusion.

"I just don't understand it," she said, still going on about Evan. "Being around dying people. Being there when they die. He told me he actually held someone in his arms at the very moment he died. Like it was this religious experience. Well, I don't get it. To me it's really . . . well, disgusting. Isn't it?"

She was wearing a tweed jacket, a blue blouse, a brown wool skirt, pearls. Everything she owned was imported, and not from Malaysia or Singapore. She lived in a rose-covered cottage worth a million bucks, far away from city dirt and crime and pain and desire. She didn't even clean her own house. She was immune to more than thrush and rampant yeast infections. She was immune to everything.

My father's thirsty ghost was still hovering around the table, summoned by the smell of wet galoshes, pipe tobacco and scotch. The ache I felt whenever I thought of him hovered around too, that feeling of failure, of lack of strength, lack of sense, whatever it was. We fucked up twice, all three of us, but Evan was the only one who was making restitution for it.

"It's been five years," I said, "since Dad died."

"I remember, Alex. Believe me, I remember."

"Do you?"

I'm sure she remembered, but differently than I did. I remembered being the only one in his room, watching this skeleton that had once been my father concentrating everything on trying to breathe. I remembered the look on the nurse's face when I left. I remembered going to the Park and sitting in the Tea Garden and finally going home. I remembered getting a phone call. He had died about an hour after I left.

And I remembered why no one else was there. Elizabeth was someplace on vacation. Evan had just gone back east to school after Christmas break, and didn't have enough money to fly home again. Our mother was already dead.

No one had been with her when she died either. I was only a kid then, but I know we were all at home when the phone call came. We had been at the hospital that afternoon and then it was dinnertime and we all left.

Which is why Evan doesn't leave anymore. He stays to the very end. He holds their hands. Sometimes he holds their whole bodies. Not that he's ever said it in so many words, but I know what's really going on. I know him. We think the same way, but, unlike me, he acts on what he thinks. I don't act; all I'm good for is regret.

"I had a Mass said for him," Elizabeth said. "Not that I go to Mass anymore myself, but I know it's something he'd want done. They've become very expensive, you know, Masses for the Dead. They used to be ten or twenty dollars. Now . . ."

"Look, I have to go," I said, nearly jumping out of my seat. "Sorry, Elizabeth, I just remembered I have to be somewhere in fifteen minutes."

I leaned over and kissed her. She wasn't expecting such sisterly tenderness. She jumped too and almost knocked over her coffee and Grand Marnier.

I had to be outside. I had to be in the rain. I had to go to the corner of Liberty and Noe and take a look at those stairs. Because I used to live near there, off Noe, and I used to go up and down those stairs and I could almost swear that they had landings, that it would be impossible for someone to fall all the way from the top to the bottom. The landings would stop you.

Because all of a sudden I knew what Evan was doing at the AIDS hospice. And all of a sudden I knew that it was OK to substitute, to do something for a person because you should have done it for someone else but couldn't or didn't. That it was the doing that mattered, even if the person you were doing it for wasn't the right person, your mother, say, or your brother, the person you might be morally obliged to act for, the person you weren't ready to act for when they needed you to act.

It was a bizarre illogical sort of logic that I had in my head as I walked in the rain over to my bus stop on Market Street. I needed to hold onto the thought, though, the idea. I didn't want to lose it. I made it into a kind of mantra, so I could keep it clear: If I were Jeff Taylor's sister, I wouldn't rest until I found out what happened to him. So until Jeff Taylor's sister shows up, I'm going to do her work for her.

On the night of Tuesday, January 19th, or in the early morning hours of Wednesday, January 20th, a black gay florist, age thirty-five, was stabbed and beaten to death in his condo off Buena Vista Park.

On the night of Thursday, January 21st, between 10:30 and midnight, a white gay enumerator, age twenty-five, was killed (mugged? beaten up? thrown down the stairs?) at Liberty Street between Sanchez and Noe.

Connection between these two?

1. They knew each other
2. They were gay
3. They were involved in the AIDS Study
4. They were killed two days apart
5. They were killed in San Francisco, about one half mile from each other.

Evan, who had come in and shaken the rain out of his hair all over my page, read over my shoulder and haroomphed.

"The first three could be true of about a hundred people in this neighborhood, at least. How do you know Lamont was involved in the study?"

"Sean said he was a designated household. That's why Jeff didn't want to finish enumerating the building, because he didn't want to have to talk to him. Or something."

"So Sean did it?"

"I don't know. I mean, he never said he actually talked to Lamont, only that his apartment was one of the households in that building that somebody had to check on."

"And Jeff didn't want to do it. So Sean must have."

"Or maybe he hadn't gotten to it yet," I said. "He would have said, don't you think? If he had talked to Lamont?"

"I don't know. You know the man better than I do."

"Hardly," I said. "I haven't had that intense one-on-one discussion of my intimate sexual desires and secret proclivities with him that you have, my dear. Not yet, anyway."

Evan haroomphed again.

"Anyway," I went on, "I think it's suspicious, two gay men killed in two days. Also, Evan, I went over to Liberty Street today and checked out that staircase. If Jeff had fallen down it or been thrown down it from the top, he wouldn't have fallen all the way down. There are stairs and then landings, pretty big ones, five or so. I don't think he could have possibly gone all the way down from the top."

Evan just raised his eyebrows and went to change his clothes. But he came out of his room about thirty seconds later.

"Zand, I hope you're not thinking about messing around with this . . ."

"I don't have anything else to do," I said. "And even you said that Lamont was a great person and they should catch the . . ."

"Zand," he said. "That's what the cops are for."

"Really? I thought the cops were for giving tickets to jaywalkers and arresting aggressive panhandlers."

He retired into his room again, re-emerged after another half-minute.

"I don't want you doing this."

"What? Doing what? Thinking?"

"Thinking about this. I know you. You get in trouble. Easily."

"Funny. That's just what Elizabeth said about you today."

"That I get in trouble?"

"That she didn't approve of what you were doing at the hospice. Dangerous. Disgusting. You could catch the virus from bedpans or something."

"Poor Elizabeth," he said.

"Don't you know a cop, Evan?"

"I know the harbor patrol. That's about as close to cops . . . No, actually, I do know a cop. I dated a cop. Three years ago though. And briefly. Too macho for my taste."

"Could this cop be persuaded to tell you anything about . . ."

"That's homicide. My cop was in traffic control. I bet I could get you information on all their parking tickets."

"Where do you meet cops anyway?"

"I met my cop over a speeding ticket on the Embarcadero."

"Then where did you go?"

"Her place." He smiled at me angelically. "This isn't going to work, Zand."

"We'll see about that," I said. "They would tell his lover, wouldn't they? How he died exactly. Stuff like that."

"A random act of violence. And Lamont was killed by a trick. They'll catch the trick, I'll bet. But Jeff . . . I mean, people are killed in this town everyday and nobody ever finds out . . ."

"I'm going to find out," I said. "At least I want to find out if it was really as random as you think it was."

"The mugger asked him for his wallet. He didn't produce it fast enough, so the mugger hit him. He fell down the stairs and broke his neck. That's what you're going to find out. But, you know, if it keeps you off the job market, by all means."

"I'm meeting Sean for a beer later on. He'll know something."

"Watch out for that guy."

"Why?"

"Because if it turns out that he did talk to Lamont, then he's the one direct link between Lamont's murder and Jeff's. Maybe what we're dealing with here, Alexandra, is a *serial* killer."

Evan should drop environmental science for stand-up comedy. He's such a riot.

CHAPTER 5

Sean was walking close to me, closer than he had all night. Talking in that low, gentle voice of his, intimate, like a lover's voice. Talking about death.

"There's sort of a silence at the University now," he was saying. "Like everyone's in shock. They've been doing these kinds of studies for years and nothing like this has ever happened. I mean, take me. I've enumerated in the projects, in the Mission, Valencia Gardens, lower Haight, Divisidero and Fell, out there 9, 10 at night, sometimes interviews end after 11, I've never run into any trouble. And I've walked into places with some pretty wild people, you know. Maybe somebody tells me to fuck off, or eyeballs me on the street. But nothing's ever happened to me. Nothing's happened to any of the women either. Ever. This is the first casualty. But of course they're saying he wasn't working for the study at the time. It was much too late for him to be enumerating and he wasn't scheduled for an interview, so the study's off the hook, at least legally. Morally, well, that's another question."

"Morally? What do you mean?"

"He was going to meet that paranoid respondent, the one I told you about, remember? He was going by his house after I dropped him off to give it one more shot. But I can't tell them that. Confidentiality and all."

"Even so, Sean. It was almost midnight."

We were on the streets ourselves and it was almost midnight, but I've never been afraid walking around San Francisco and I had no intention of getting afraid now. We were also in my neighborhood, walking up Castro from Haight Street where we'd been drinking beer and smoking cigarettes and talking about everything on earth but murder.

Until now.

He had to talk to someone, I guess. Eventually.

He had tried to talk to Jeff's lover, but the phone was always busy. He had tried to get information from his supervisor, Lydia, but all she had told him was that Jeff's pack must have been taken because she couldn't locate some of his enumeration folders and interviews. She had asked his roommate to look for them. Maybe they'd turn up.

"But since Jeff's roommate was his lover," Sean said, "I'm not sure finding those interviews is his major priority right now."

We walked for awhile without speaking. I had avoided bringing up this subject all evening, hoping he would talk about it without a prompt. He hadn't. Maybe he thought I wasn't interested. Maybe he thought I was more interested in his trip to China, my own year in Taos, the war in Bosnia, anything but what may have happened to Jeff Taylor and Lamont Bliss. And I didn't want to scare him off by asking directly. I know how intimidating I can be with men, how easily they get spooked.

But now that the subject had come up, I had to restrain myself. Stay cool, Alexandra, I cautioned myself. Don't trip.

"Do men usually carry their wallets in their back packs?" I asked with as much indifference as I could muster.

"Maybe some men do. I wouldn't. Why?"

"Well, the paper said his wallet wasn't taken. Lydia thinks they took his pack. But I just wondered if a mugger would bother with a pack. It seems strange to me."

He didn't say anything, so I pressed on.

"Another thing is that Liberty Street above Sanchez is really quiet. It's at the top of a hill, it's a dead end, too, except for that little alley. Why would a mugger look for someone to rob up there at that hour? I mean, how would a mugger even get up there, when you think about it. It's a good climb."

"OK. Go on."

"Well, I'm just thinking. What if he was killed somewhere else and dumped at the bottom of those stairs? A car-jacking, maybe. I mean, it would make more sense that he was thrown out of a car than thrown down the stairs. If he was thrown at all."

We walked and walked. We were headed more or less toward my house but also toward Sanchez and Liberty. In that direction. We weren't going there exactly, we were just oriented that way. Toward Castro and Market. Then up Castro, to 18th, where Lamont's florist shop was. Along 18th to Noe. Up Noe to the stairs at Liberty. Up the stairs. Then we'd be there.

It was quite a hike.

"Why are you thinking about this?" He sounded almost as stern as Evan.

"No reason," I said, covering my tracks as coolly as possible.

"Everybody in San Francisco thinks in conspiracies. Everything's a conspiracy. Nothing can just happen. There are no accidents in San Francisco. This whole town's based on there not being any accidents. It's all a plot."

I backed off fast and started talking about the last movie I'd seen, which had nothing to do with anything except that it had a good plot.

He walked me home, where he had left his car, and we said goodnight and that was that.

Evan was up reading about impermanence. He gave me the news update in return for my last cigarette: Robert Slatley, only son of the queen of the Christian right in America, had just come out. On Inauguration Day. Right here in San Francisco. Gee whiz.

"He was going to be outed," Evan added after I distinctly disappointed him by not being entirely overjoyed by this event. "So he called a reporter from the *Chronicle* and just told him."

"Big deal," I said. "Who cares?"

"A lot of people. A lot of people would rather have seen him dive off the Golden Gate than talk to the *Chronicle*. If you ask me, he's lucky he's alive."

I woke up Saturday morning with the phone ringing in my ear. It was a familiar voice, but I was still asleep so it was a bit hard to identify right off. The voice said, "I got something in the mail you gotta see. I'm coming over, OK?"

I said fine and went back to sleep.

He threw a manila envelope on the table and poured himself a cup of coffee.

"It's cold," I said as he gagged on it. I hadn't been up long enough to make coffee or warm up the leftovers. Sean looked distraught. I put up a kettle of water.

"Just look," he said.

I sat down and opened the envelope. "Dirty pictures?" I asked, half thinking that's exactly what they would be.

It was one of the survey interviews. Just one. A yellow stick-on note on the front. "Hi Sean. Please hold on to this for me. I'll explain later. Thanks. Jeff."

"Read it," he said.

"I thought it was all confidential and everything."

"It is," he said. "I'm breaking confidentiality, OK? I have to. This is too scary for me and you already have a conspiracy theory in the works, don't you?"

"Always," I said and tried to smile at him. He was looking a little green. "Sit down. Have some coffee, in a minute. Have some toast."

"Please read it," he said. "I need some sanity."

It was sweet that he thought I could represent sanity in his life.

I sat down and started to read.

It was all in the verbatim.

All along the sides of the pages, in all the margins, in the lines between the questions.

Jeff's handwriting was small, precise, perfectly legible, a form indifferent to content. It didn't change the way I had noticed Sean's did; it didn't tire, show emotion, judge. It just recorded—everything.

It took me a long time to read it. While I read Sean made coffee and scrambled eggs. I devoured mine without taking my eyes off the pages.

When I was finished reading, I closed the interview form and looked across the table at him. He must have read something on my face because he came over to me and kissed me, very tenderly, very gently. Then not so tenderly or gently. Pretty soon we were pulling off each other's clothes.

"Oh, God, Alexandra," he said, "let's go to bed."

The proximity of sex and death.

I don't think it's something we know how to talk about yet. It's something we know with our bodies. It's some kind of physical logic. It defies words.

We had sex, very safe sex, but sex nonetheless, like two people who had just escaped drowning. Fucking right on the sand, within inches of the sea. Fuck you, death, we say. We're still breathing. Watch us survive you.

And then, having fucked death, we made love to each other.

We didn't mention Jeff's name again until afternoon. Not that we forgot about him. I certainly couldn't, kissing the skull tattoo over Sean's heart.

"Why do you think he sent it to you?" I asked him while we were foraging in the refrigerator for beers. The interview was still lying on the kitchen table.

"I knew there was something he wasn't telling me. I thought he was worried . . ."

"Scared. You said scared."

"Did I?"

"Yes. You said you thought he had a premonition."

"He was too involved. He was too concerned. Me, I would have just talked to Lydia and let her deal with it. That's her job."

"You turn over the interview to her at your review?"

"Once a week. A grueling process it is, too. Hard on the nerves."

"When was his review?"

"I don't know. Mondays maybe."

"So would he have had a review last Monday? It was a holiday."

"Probably not. She'd reschedule it, though. Why?"

"Because this interview was done on the fourteenth. He held onto it an extra week."

"It's possible he missed a review this week. Shit."

"Because Lydia would have known what to do?"

"Well, I don't know if she would have known what to do, but at least Jeff wouldn't have had it."

"He didn't have it anyway. He sent it to you."

We sat at the table, naked, drinking our beers. Outside

gay men were walking up and down the street, going to brunch or coming back, shopping, doing the laundry. Some women, too, from the sound of voices coming through the windows. The idea struck me that in all of the Castro, Sean might well be the only straight man sitting stark naked at a kitchen table. That he was unique in this respect made me love him even more.

The proximity of sex and death.

One of us had to say it sooner or later, and since it was my house and my table, my bed, my beer, I suppose it was up to me to be the one. So I said it.

"Somebody killed him for this interview."

We both looked at the white folder, Confidential Information stamped in black all over it.

"Maybe we're just trippin' over this," he said.

He didn't sound convinced.

CHAPTER 6

The AIDS study interview was about thirty pages long. The respondent's name did not appear on it. The respondent was identified by number only.

The first group of questions involved the respondent's health. This respondent's health was good. He was not HIV positive, at least not as of his last test six months earlier. He had had bouts with other venereal diseases, the common garden type varieties: herpes, gonorrhea, syphilis.

The next set of questions involved sexual experiences and activity.

The respondent identified himself as gay. Unlike "a lot

of people I could name," he was out to almost everybody he knew. He went to gay bars regularly, a few times a week. Over the past twelve months he had engaged in sexual intercourse with approximately (approximately because, he said, he had probably missed a few of the less memorable ones as he was counting up) thirty-five different men. Over the past five years he had engaged in sexual intercourse with about—this was a real ball park figure—three hundred different men. He had never engaged in sexual intercourse with a woman.

The next group of questions asked specific questions about sexual activity, how many times it occurred and with how many partners over the past twelve months, and how many times a condom was used with each partner and each activity. These questions were posed first from the perspective of the active partner and then from the perspective of the passive partner. They formed a sort of litany of homosexual possibility, from masturbation, through oral intercourse, active and passive, to anal intercourse active and passive, with ejaculation or without, with condom or without, how many partners, how many times. You had to have a good memory for this interview, or else a good imagination.

The same questions were repeated for heterosexuals, but without the passive questions. Heterosexual intercourse had fewer possibilities.

There followed questions about use of drugs and alcohol, injection of recreational drugs, how many times the respondent had been high while having sex, whether the respondent had been paid for sex over the past year. There were questions about how many people the respondent knew with AIDS or who were HIV positive. There were questions about how the respondent felt other people viewed safe sex practices and how he himself felt about them. There were several pages of questions about a primary relationship, if one existed.

Finally there were demographical questions—ethnicity, education, income, employment, home state, date of birth.

It wasn't the easily coded single word or number answers to the questions that were of interest. It was the additional information, the running commentary, the personal revelations that this respondent had blurted out and that Jeff had dutifully recorded that made this particular interview so compelling.

It was as though he had to tell someone and Jeff was listening and writing everything down.

"He was just one of those people you open up to," Sean said. Late afternoon, getting dark already, and I was re-reading the interview and commenting on how much the respondent had talked, non-stop it seemed, all the way through it. "I mean, if I had a problem, he's the kind of person I'd tell, you know? All you had to do is sit down with him and you'd feel better. He had that soothing kind of vibe."

"I thought you only knew him from training."

"Yeah. Well, we had dinner together a few times too. Once just the two of us and once with Monica. She's another enumerator. We were trying to hang out together a little. It's so impersonal, working alone all the time, not being able to talk about it with anyone."

"So you were friends?"

"Yeah," he said, like he wanted to drop the subject.

"What's his lover like?"

"He's a cook. They went to high school together. One of those long-term relationships. Moved here together from Michigan. I liked him."

"So you've met him?"

"We went out drinking one night, the three of us. Why are you asking?"

"You could ask him about the coroner's report."

"Could I?"

"Well, you're going to call him anyway, right? You could just ask."

Sean looked miserable, so I didn't push it. They were friends. That explained a lot.

I thought Evan was the only straight man on earth who actually had gay friends.

I guess I don't know as much about men as I thought.

"But didn't you say he was involved with Lamont?" I asked, suddenly remembering that conversation.

"Jeff? Did I?"

"Yes. You said that's why he didn't finish enumerating on Buena Vista Park."

"Well, yeah. I guess I did say that."

"So what about his long-term relationship?"

"Long-term doesn't mean monogamous. Jeff and Brendan have been together since they were seventeen. That's eight years. No one's monogamous for eight years."

"Oh," I said. "Stupid me."

"Maybe there are rare exceptions," he said quickly, trying to placate me, not sure about what exactly I was bristling about, the news itself or the tone in which he delivered it.

"Hmm," I said, not sure myself. "I wonder how he felt when Lamont's name popped up here."

"It's a small town. You'd expect names to pop up."

And Mr. Respondent X had sure popped up with a lot of them.

It was all in the verbatim.

The verbatim started with the health questions and

moved right along, deeper and deeper into this man's life, his lovers' lives, their sexual obsessions, his reactions.

He knew a lot of men.

He'd had sex with a lot of men.

A lot of closeted men.

A lot of important closeted men.

And he just couldn't help telling Jeff all about it.

And Jeff had written it all down.

"I'm out. Way out. Out all the time, to everyone. Not like some people I could name. You know, the ones who think it's dirty. I love those guys. They fuck you and then they spit all over you. They suck your dick and then go back to their straight lives and talk about how gays are disgusting. Like they're not. I mean, we aren't disgusting. They're disgusting. And, you know, I don't know what they think they're doing either because it's like we don't have brains or something. We let them fuck us in bed and then fuck us on the news. Oh, yeah, I've been with men like that. It should scare the shit out of them, what I know about them. Do they think I'm going to keep quiet all my life? Do they think I'm that stupid?"

This was only page 5.

A few pages later, the question: Did anyone pay you to have sexual intercourse with them?

"Oh, they don't pay me for sex. They pay me to keep quiet about it. Oh, they pay for that. Never come right out and say it, but it's like a bribe, you know? It's like, You need rent money? You need a new car? It's like, You understand that I can't take you out for dinner, so let me pay your Visa bill. That kind of shit."

But the names had started coming out before that. How old were you the very first time you had sexual intercourse with another man? "Thirteen. No, twelve. I was twelve. Father Joseph Daly. Seduced by the altar boy. I was in love with the man, but then I found out he was seduced by a lot of altar boys. Poor guy."

By page 9 names were slipping out all over the place. The ones who used three condoms because they were so scared of getting sick. The ones who made him wear condoms because he was gay, but never wore them themselves because they weren't. The ones who would never get beyond masturbation because they were so scared. The ones who just liked dressing up. The ones who made him dress up.

He had entertained a wide range of men over the past twelve months. The florist, Lamont Bliss, was one of them. ("I wasn't quite trashy enough for Lamont, though. He liked his boys down and out, hungry and vicious. He liked to drive his big black Jag down to Mission and Van Ness and pluck them up off the street. Noblesse oblige, darling. Feed and fondle. He likes danger, Lamont. He likes them dangerous.") Actors whose names I recognized. A few local businessmen. A bunch of naval officers from Treasure Island. ("No gays in the military. What a joke. I could tell you about gays in the military. Top brass. Speaking from personal experience, though, they're not real good at what they do. I'd hate to see them trying to aim *real* missiles at anyone.") And the *pièce de résistance*, a general, recently in the news for virulently opposing any change in the military's exclusion of homosexuals, who were, so he claimed, "sexually obsessed, untrustworthy by nature, not made of the stuff real men are made of, and if present in the ranks would represent a threat and danger to those brave young men dedicated to serving their country."

I remembered this quote since it had been picked up by *The Bay Guardian* and placed in bold under the photograph of the Soldier of the Year, his chest bedecked with medals, who had just revealed that he was gay.

And was summarily discharged.

Navy brass, army generals, parish priests and the Soldier of the Year.

It was a little unnerving. Was every man alive a closet case?

Evan came home from the hospice at 5:30. I ran to the door and hugged him so tight he squeaked.

"What's this for? Did you break something?"

We used to give our parents particularly big hugs on those days they came home from work to find windows broken by baseballs, or broken dishes or broken furniture. We were a wild bunch, but we knew the power of the hug.

"I'm just glad you're home," I said. "And we need you."

"We?" Then he noticed Sean sitting shirtless and tattooed at the kitchen table, and the full ashtray and the empty beer bottles. He noticed the white interview form too. "Oh," he said, which suggested to me that he got the whole picture all at once, sex, death, murder, lust, passion, terror, confusion, remorse, and that I loved him more than he realized because he was a man with soul and what we needed now was soul and smarts and insight and also dinner, which it was his turn to make.

CHAPTER 7

Evan's idea of Saturday night dinner: pasta, bread and butter, milkshakes, beer. I don't know how we stay skinny in this house. It must be urban stress, nerves, intestinal worms, whatever they put in the water. Agua Slim, or something.

Since he had asked ("Anything going on here I should know about?"), we told him everything over dinner. Almost everything. What we didn't tell him, he figured out. Evan is quick like that.

"It's interesting all right," he said when we had finished. "But how is this your problem? That's what I don't understand."

"It's not a *problem*, Evan," I said, at the same moment Sean said, "Once we turn the interview in . . ."

"What happens?"

"It's gone. Out of reach. Nobody except the inner circle will ever see it again."

"OK. So give it to the police."

"Oh, God, Evan!" I said, at the same moment Sean said, "And lose my job?"

"You gotta stop talking in stereo," my brother groaned, getting himself another beer. "Why would you lose your job? There's been a murder, after all. If you think this interview is evidence . . ."

"Man, they fire us even for talking to each other about respondents. The whole study is based on everything being confidential. It's the Prime Directive, you know? We have to sign all these documents promising to maintain confidentiality. It's drilled into us. How sensitive the documents are. How important the trust factor is. How the information we're collecting is so vital. Tracking the infection rate. Discovering if sexual practices have changed. Ten years of work designing it and umpteen million dollars funding it and lives depending on it and blah blah blah. Jesus, Evan, I'd get fired in a heartbeat, and it took me six months to get this job. Besides, just practically speaking, the interview doesn't mean shit to anyone unless you know that Jeff was the interviewer and that he was going to see this guy the night he was killed and that the guy had been bugging him about getting this back. For what appear to be obvious reasons."

"And how do you know this?"

"He told me. That night. We had coffee together."

"But he must have already mailed you the interview, right? He didn't tell you he'd sent it to you? When was it postmarked?"

"Thursday. So, yeah, he had to have already mailed it."

"Why didn't he say so?"

"I don't know."

"And why did he mail it to you and not to the University?"

"Evan," I said. "He doesn't know, OK? How could he know?"

"Well?" Evan said to Sean, completely ignoring me. "Any idea?"

Sean lit a cigarette, the last one in the house. I knew he was trying to work something out, but I got the feeling that whatever it was, he was resisting it. Sometimes things are just too heavy to think about.

"Like I said to Alex, I think he knew that something might happen to him." He spoke slowly, measuring every word. "I guess he just couldn't tell me. Maybe he was afraid I'd think he was crazy or being melodramatic. Maybe he just didn't trust me enough. Or maybe he made it real clear and I just didn't *hear* him, you know? Maybe I wasn't really listening to him. And if nothing had happened after all, then he'd call me today and ask if I got it and apologize for bothering me and tell me he was stressed out but everything's fine now . . ."

"So what do you think happened to him?"

"I think," I said, before anybody got too out of control, "that we need to find this respondent and talk to him."

"Tell him his confidential interview has been read?" Sean asked. "Great idea."

"No. You could go and see him and tell him Jeff isn't with the study anymore and you're taking over his cases—I mean, this is true, right? And that Jeff left a notation or something on the interview that the respondent wanted to be contacted again, or something like that. To clarify the interview. Don't you do that sometimes if things aren't clear?"

"Yeah. Sure. We go back. We call. I can go and see him and ask what he wanted from Jeff. Yeah, I can do that. If I can find him."

"Can you?"

"I have his ID number. If I had Jeff's enumeration folders, I could find him in a pinch. But Lydia says the folders are missing. Maybe they're at his house. Maybe they got stolen. Who knows where they are."

He had that truly melancholy look on his face again. Evan gets that look a lot too. This must be how it is to live during wartime, or through a terror. People disappear on you. Your friends. People you know casually. People you love. This was why I left San Francisco in the first place. I'd forgotten, but here it was again, that sorrow at the heart of things. Soul-ache.

"But say you find him," Evan said. "And say you ask what he wants and say he says to you what he said to Jeff, that he wants the interview back, or changed, or whatever. I still don't get it. What do you think you'll find out? You gonna ask him if he pushed Jeff down the stairs because he wouldn't give him back his interview? Or are you gonna wait and see if he tries getting it from you?"

Evan had finally said out loud what I at least had been thinking all night: if this respondent had in fact pushed Jeff down the stairs or whatever to get the interview back, and then taken his pack to see if it was in there, if he was that intent on retrieving this interview, the last thing Sean should do is let him know that it was still out in the world, retrievable. And not just out in the world, floating in the void, but specifically sitting on my kitchen table, or on Sean's.

"Another thing I don't understand," Evan said, screwing up his face while he poured his beer and watched it overflow onto the table top. "I don't understand why Jeff didn't just clean it up. Like if it was the names he was worried about, big deal, just cross them out."

"We're not supposed to erase things. Yeah, we can put a line through them, but they're never really unreadable."

"He couldn't have whited them out?"

"No. He'd get fired."

"Well, getting fired sure as hell beats getting killed."

"I don't think he saw it as that kind of choice," Sean said.

"No. Right. Well, then. What's the plan?"

We sat around listening to the foam on our beer pop, wishing for cigarettes—or at least I was wishing. I could go get some, though Evan would lecture me, explain how important it is to be able to keep breathing, how many people wish they could keep breathing, if only for just one more day.

"Maybe Evan should read it and see what he thinks?" I said. "One more head at work."

"Sure," Sean said sounding dismal. "Why not? Read it if you want. Maybe you'll see something in it we missed."

Evan's good at puzzles. And it would keep him occupied. Maybe reading about all that meaningless sex would make him feel less miserable about his spending another Saturday night at home with no date.

We left Evan with the interview and went to the movies.

I needed to be transported, I didn't care where. We wound up someplace in Italy about a hundred years ago, in a villa with some English women, falling in love.

We were going to wind up falling in love anyway, no matter where we were. Or at least, from the look of things, I was.

I liked that he put his arm around me when we walked. I liked the way his body felt. I liked that he didn't talk all the time. I liked the way he smelt.

Dumb reasons to fall in love with somebody, I know. I think I liked his mind too, what I'd seen of it.

He had to enumerate in the morning. Sunday morning was a good time in some neighborhoods, he told me, though not in others, mine for example. He asked me if I would like to come to his place. He lived in the Haight, on Parnassus, with two roommates who were never home. One in fact wasn't even in the country; the other had a girlfriend in the East Bay and stayed over there every weekend.

We were drifting in that direction anyway, and I think it's important to check out a man's house before you get too entangled. See what he reads. What he puts on the walls. What's in the refrigerator. What he keeps for pets.

Men who keep rats, for example, are out of my league. Also snakes. Not that I have anything against snakes, but I wouldn't want to fall in love with someone who fed little furry live animals to his pet on a regular basis.

Also we were stopping every block or so to kiss in a pretty outrageous display of heterosexual privilege which I have to admit to indulging in whenever possible.

I really liked the way Sean kissed.

We went to his place on Parnassus. We got there at about 1.

His house was in the back. It was dark in the alley, but it didn't bother me until it bothered him. I could feel him tighten up, hesitate. He was looking down the alley into the garden in his front yard.

"Something's wrong," he whispered.

"What?" I whispered back.

"There should be a light. In the garden. It's on a timer. It should be on."

There was night-blooming jasmine somewhere around, in the garden perhaps. Its scent was intoxicating. But Sean was worried about the light. He had stopped dead in his tracks. "I don't like this," he said.

I wanted to say, Don't trip. The light's burnt out.

I didn't.

I put my arms around him and kissed him.

I get scared of the dark sometimes too. And no friend of mine was recently murdered in cold blood on a dark street.

By the time I stopped kissing him, the question of the light didn't matter anymore.

CHAPTER 8

Sean got up in the morning and went off to enumerate; I slept on. I slept and dreamt.

In the middle of my dream the phone next to the bed rang. It rang a lot. It kept ringing.

I woke up just as the recording clicked off.

A male voice said: "Hi, Sean. This is Gray. Listen, I'm sorry, but I can't meet you tonight. It's getting complicated. *We're* getting complicated, you know? I want to talk. I want to try to work this out. But I can't do it tonight. I have to go see my parents, and . . . Look, I'll be home after ten. Why don't you call, OK?"

I lay in Sean's bed looking out the window at the trees in his garden. I kept drifting off, but the phone rang three more times within the next hour until it finally drove me out of bed and into the shower.

One of the calls was from a woman named Isabel, sorry she hadn't caught him in, inviting him to an opening at some gallery on Fillmore.

One of the calls was from a woman named Monica, saying that she was calling about Jeff's memorial service, giving the date and time, asking him to get back to her, leaving her number.

The last caller didn't identify himself by name. I guess his voice was his ID.

"Hey, Sean. Listen, thanks for calling all those times. I'm sorry I wasn't able to talk. It's truly out of control here, I don't know what the fuck I'm doing, but I need to tell you this . . . I never had that conversation with him after all. So, see, he never knew. Hope that makes you feel better. Anyway, I'm doing OK and I'd like to see you . . . I miss you . . ."

I took my shower and made coffee. I made myself eggs. He actually had food in his refrigerator. I was impressed.

The first few weeks I was living with Evan I would listen to our messages and wonder how many different women Jake was dating. Then I found out they were all clients with sexy voices, or waitresses wanting him to switch shifts. Jake's a graphic designer when he's not waiting tables at Greens.

Evan has men calling him all the time. Not so much from work as from the hospice. And lovers, friends, and relatives of men in the hospice. And widowers of men who were in the hospice. They all need to talk to him and they all sound very sexy except the ones who sound very very ill.

So, yes, it might have been possible to put a different spin on those two calls, but I was buying the most overt.

There are many possibilities in the world. Some people pick one right off; other people have to check them all out or as many as they can before one of them becomes compelling. I myself have checked out a lot of them, though my imagination has very definite limits. Or maybe it's my nerve that has limits. I can imagine a lot more than I'd ever do.

Though getting involved with a bisexual man was never one of my major masochistic fantasies.

I was sitting in the living room by the window, thinking about all this and sipping my third cup of coffee when the door opened and a man came strolling in. He looked surprised to see me; I was surprised to see him.

"Hi," I said, "you must be Sean's roommate, the one who's never here."

He was a real hard-core head-banger type, pierced, tattooed, grungy, hair shaved down practically to the skin. It was a cool morning, but all he was wearing was a t-shirt and torn jeans and engineer boots. He looked like he had just rolled out of somebody's bed where he hadn't done much sleeping.

"Who are you?" he asked, looking around like he'd never seen the place before.

"A friend of Sean's. Alex."

"So. Can I get some of that coffee?" And he went into the kitchen.

I didn't see him for a long time. The bathroom was off the kitchen, and the bedrooms too. I figured he had just gone into his and crashed out.

About twenty minutes later he reappeared, looking pretty much the same. He came right up to the chair I was sitting in, and squatted down in front of me. I noticed that his nails were bitten way down, and that his hands and forearms had deep cuts all over them, some healed, some still open. Among the tattoos on his arm was one I'd never seen on anyone before, four simple but horrifying signs: HIV+.

He was one of those wiry men, the ones who are much stronger than you'd think. Younger than I'd taken him for at first too. His energy was a little weird, though. He was too close to me and he was looking at me as though he wasn't sure exactly what I was—an inanimate object or dinner.

"When's Sean coming back?"

"About 2, he said."

"I can't wait. Tell him I'll see him next time."

"Will he know when that is?"

"He'll know when he sees me." He straightened up a little and put his left hand on the arm of the chair like he was going to hold on to it while he stood up. Instead he leaned forward, put his right hand on my breast, squeezed it hard, and started sucking on my neck.

I was taken by surprise and he was hurting me on top of it, so I yelped and pushed him away as hard as I could. He backed off, but it wasn't because of my upper body strength.

"Don't want to slide, baby?" he said, but there was mockery in his voice and he was already up and walking toward the door. "I left my calling card. Check it out. And tell him I'll find him. Soon."

The second the door shut behind him, I ran over to it and put on the chain lock. Then I locked all the windows, too.

Locking the barn door, they call it.

He had been in Sean's bedroom.

Drawers were pulled open. Papers on the desk had

been gone through, moved around. My bag had been emptied. Wallet opened, credit cards and IDs scattered along with everything else on the floor, cash gone.

But the thing that sent chills up me was the bed.

He had been in it.

He had left blood on the sheets. Blood and cum.

It didn't surprise me much when Sean came home an hour later and told me that one of his roommates was a woman and the other one's name was Lin Wei Chao.

CHAPTER 9

Sunday afternoon in late January, walking the streets with Sean. We are both wearing our basic black and our moods are on the dark side, too, but the sun is shining brightly, it's 66 degrees, everybody's out strolling around, windows are wide open, music coming from everywhere. We may not feel it, but winter's over.

We walked down to Haight Street, took Masonic to the Panhandle, strolled along with everyone else on the grass. We stopped to watch a group practicing some martial art or other, another bunch playing horseshoes, kids just throwing balls around. A joint was being smoked nearby, the smell wafting to us on the slight breeze.

"Thanks for not calling the cops, by the way," he said, as though we had been talking about this subject all afternoon.

"I never call the cops. It's against my religion."

"Thanks for not asking any questions."

"Like for example?"

"Like for example, why I'm glad you didn't call the cops."

"I actually thought he might have been your roommate. Or a friend."

"A psycho-killer buddy. Everybody has one, right?"

"And he's yours?"

"No, Alex. I don't know who the hell he is. Yet."

We lay down on the grass in the park for a while, dozing until we could feel the sun going down. Then we zig-zagged our way east. On Hayes between Central and Lyon there's a Baptist Church and it was in full session. A woman was singing Gospel in a most beautiful deep voice that could be heard up and down the block. Two doors away from the Church, a long-haired white man was fixing his motorcycle, rock and roll blasting out his front windows. Around the corner on Lyon an old black man was sitting on his front steps sipping a can of beer and listening to the blues on his tape player. It was a musical sort of afternoon.

And everywhere we walked people smiled at us and said hello, or whassup? to Sean, how's it goin' baby to me. Cars politely stopped for us when we stepped into the crosswalks. Kids grinned at us as they rode by on their bikes.

We hit Divisidero at Fulton, turned south as twilight fell.

We had been walking through one of the few integrated neighborhoods in the city, but Divisidero around Fulton, Hayes, and Fell had a rough feel to it. This was one of Sean's neighborhoods; he had been enumerating here and farther east around Fell and Fillmore all morning. He'd been enumerating in this neighborhood so long, people on the street actually knew him. He told me that farther down Fell, around Webster and Buchanan, even the drug dealers knew him, the runners and the kids who watched the corners, the prostitutes.

Dusk brought the teenage boys out onto the street, all of them wearing big black jackets with their sweatshirt hoods pulled up over their heads, all of them congregating on the corners, twenty, thirty strong. As it got darker, more would come out. And the streetlights in the city were all set on dim, the whole city seemed darker these nights than usual, than I remembered it. There had been a rash of car-jackings in this neighborhood, people shot dead getting in or out of their cars or thrown out of them at high speeds. A local musician had been killed on the Panhandle one night while he was walking his dog. People smoked crack right out on the sidewalks, shot up in doorways. After dark whole sections of certain streets became impassable, the sidewalks covered storefront to curb with people sleeping on the pavement because they had no other place to go. In these neighborhoods, houses were secured with every kind of gate and lock imaginable; every window had bars. Going home must have felt like going to jail, except the bars and locks and gates weren't to keep you in, but to keep them out.

In the year I'd been gone, the city had changed.

We got to Divisidero and Haight and turned east.

Haight between Steiner and Fillmore. A mix of poor blacks, young whites, homeless people, drug dealers, prostitutes, punks, queers, women on motorcycles, men in chains, bookstores, cafés, bars, street vendors, tattoo parlors—in that one block you could find just about anything: crack, S and M sex, decaffeinated lattes—anything.

We were looking for something there too.

We went into one of the funky, smoke-filled cafés and got a couple of cappuccinos. I felt old and respectable in this place. Under-pierced. Well dressed. It made me nervous.

A character out of a punk version of James Fenimore Cooper, multi-pierced, in buckskins and beads, thigh-high suede boots, a blonde mohawk, sauntered over to our table, pulled up a chair and sat down.

"You're back," she said.

"Yeah," Sean answered. "What's up?"

"Not much," she said. "What do you need?"

"A gang-banger with an armful of tattoos, one of them an HIV positive. A little random. Takes things."

"Trouble," she said. "Very outside."

"Can I find him?"

"You don't want to find him."

"Say I do."

"I got some nice . . ."

"Not tonight."

"She with you?"

"Alexandra," he said.

The woman nodded at me. "Shira."

"Hi," I said, feeling like a window ornament.

Shira sighed and pulled a smoke from somewhere inside her clothes. "Fuller," she said. "Bad news."

"Where do I find him?"

"You get in your nice silver Mercedes and you cruise up and down the street, and you know what? He'll find you."

"He's a dealer?"

"He's a hustler. Big time."

She smoked her smoke, not tobacco, some herbal weed or other. She was striking, completely exposed with her shaved head and pierced face, every feature out in the open. Hers were elegant, classical; even the shape and color of her eyes stood out clear and defined. Prince Valiant in buckskins, female version.

"They all get what they deserve," she said, a little sadly. "The ones he goes with, they deserve him. He deserves them. He'll die on this street. Karma."

"This street," he said.

"Yeah. Let's get off it."

We walked back up Haight to Divisidero where a left turn would start us on our way back to the Castro. After the darkness and weirdness of Haight, the Castro was going to feel as cheerful and safe as Santa's Village.

But Sean didn't turn at the corner.

"Where are we going?" I asked him.

"We have to talk," he said.

That much was true.

Buena Vista Park is on a hill. At the foot of the hill is Haight Street, at the top is Buena Vista, East and West, dominated by the huge pink building that was once a children's hospital, now very upscale condos. The park itself is a combination of grass and woods, a place to cruise, run your dogs, do drugs or sleep. From the top of the hill on a clear day, you can see the Golden Gate. On the other side of Buena Vista, smaller hills roll down toward the Castro, though Acid Hill, otherwise known as Corona Heights, stands up stark and bald and distinct among them. From the top of Acid Hill, it seems that the whole city lies at your feet, and, unlike other such spots in the city, it's an easy climb.

We bought beer and cigarettes and headed, along with the homeless, the drunk, the drugged and the sexually obsessed, to Buena Vista Park.

We sat on a bench facing the former hospital, a huge pink stucco building with a red tile roof, a chapel in back and the Baby Jesus over the front door, watching lights go on inside, stars pop out overhead, listening to the trees murmur behind us.

"OK," I said, taking a bottle from him and a light, "I'm ready. Let's talk."

"Something strange is going on in my life," he said. "I'm not sure what it is."

He sounded so sorrowful. I wanted to hold his hand, but my hands were full. So I just sat still and waited.

"I'm in trouble that I can't tell you about, Alex. Maybe this guy knows about it. I have to talk to him."

"This guy . . . Fuller?"

"The one who attacked you. If he is Fuller."

"Attack may be too strong a word," I said. "Robbed is more like it."

"He might have hurt you. He might have killed you."

We were repeating the conversation we had had earlier at his house. Except then he had been holding me and I had felt a lot better than I did now.

Even then we hadn't known what to say about the bed. I had shown him; he had stripped the sheets off and thrown them in the back hall. I wasn't sure it was supposed to be a message or anything, but I couldn't help think that leaving blood and cum on a sheet is sort of the late twentieth-century version of the black spot. So now I said, "Sean, he came in your bed. What does that mean?"

"I don't know," he said. "Maybe it doesn't mean anything. Maybe he breaks into houses and jerks off in people's beds. How am I supposed to know?"

"But maybe he knows something about you? That's what you think? What do you think he knows?"

He swigged down a few long swallows of beer and set the empty neatly on the ground next to the bench. He reached into the bag and pulled out another one, twisted off the top, took another deep pull.

"Alex, listen," he said, holding the bottle around the neck like he wanted to strangle it, "I can't ask you to be with me when I can't tell you what's going on. But I can't tell you. And I don't want to ask you to trust me. It's not fair and it may be dangerous for you. It's already been dangerous for you. And anyway you barely know me. I'm not exactly the person I seem to be. I mean, I am, when I'm with you. But there's other stuff going on too. So I think we should stop seeing each other for awhile. Until this is over."

"You don't want to ask me to trust you because you're afraid I'll say no?"

"It's too much to ask."

I wanted to say, But we're lovers, aren't we? But I didn't, because I wasn't sure that lovers was exactly what we were yet.

"It's not too much to ask," I said. "If I was the one in trouble, I'd ask you."

He put his bottle down and put his arm around me. I needed that, to feel his body, lean and taut and muscular, close against mine. The soul is inside the body, after all. It's embodied, the soul. You can't tell much about it using words; you have to discover it by feel.

"Besides," I said, "you need me. I'm the one who saw him. You won't be able to ID him unless I'm there to tell you."

He held me tighter.

I hadn't told him about his phone messages. The light on his machine had been blinking; he could have noticed and listened. I hoped those calls didn't have anything to do with this trouble he was in. But there was nothing I could do about it now. Given the way the day had gone, I wasn't ready to deal with the bisexual issue on top of everything else.

"See that building?" he whispered in my ear, nodding

across the street at the former children's hospital. I couldn't miss it, big as it was and right in my face. "Top floor. That bunch of dark windows at the corner? That's where Lamont lived. That's where he was murdered. Right there."

I followed his gaze up to the top floor, to the corner windows, the dark places up there near the first stars.

"This is the building you're enumerating?"

"Yeah. Watch how people get inside. Look at this guy now at the phone by the door. He'll stand there and call up. He's dialing a three digit code on that phone. The code rings the tenant's telephone. If he's lucky, someone will answer and buzz him in. If he's not, he'll get the answering machine."

We sat on the bench and watched the man, who happened to be dressed in full leather, get buzzed in. We watched several men leave with large dogs on leashes. A mixed-sex couple left, and a same-sex couple entered, opening the door with a key. A lot of traffic for a Sunday night.

"Some of them are probably just getting up," he said, reading my mind for the first time. "Looking for a late Sunday brunch."

My eyes drifted back up to the dark northeast corner of the building.

"Lamont used to cruise Haight Street in a silver Mercedes, didn't he?"

"A black Jag, I think. But, yeah, basically."

"You don't think Fuller—" I just let it sit there, wondering if he'd fill in the blanks.

"It crossed my mind when Shira was talking, yeah. I have to find out."

"But why, Sean? What does any of this have to do with you?" I was scared to ask this question, remembering those two different but equally intense messages on his answering machine. But if we were going to trust each other, I guess I was going to have to start somewhere.

"You mean, if the man in my apartment is the same man who killed Lamont?" The idea that the man with the HIV+ tattoo who squeezed my tit could have been the man who beat Lamont Bliss to death hit me in a strange way, sent something creeping up my backbone, made my head feel like all the hair on my head was standing up on end like fur on a cat's back.

Then he said, "There's something I haven't told you. There's a lot I haven't told you, Alex. About that night."

"The night Lamont was killed?" Now I had goosebumps on top of goosebumps. But I had to know. That was the thing. I had to know.

"Yes. That night. I talked to Lamont the night he was killed. I was enumerating. I talked to him. I was inside his place. Right up there. I looked out those windows, Alex, looked right across the city to the Golden Gate. I was there . . ."

"Tuesday night?" I asked, because he had stopped and I wanted him to go on. I wanted to hear the whole story. I knew there was more. Obviously. Much more.

"That particular building is a bitch to get into," he said slowly, squinting over at it as though he was an archeologist and the building was an ancient Mayan pyramid he had spent half his life trying to figure out. "I'd been going there for weeks trying to get inside. See, our enumeration folders don't show apartment codes. We're supposed to be enumerating certain addresses. In a building like this, we have certain apartments to go to. Apartment 301, say, or 510. But you go to that directory outside the front door there, you don't see a list of names and apartment numbers. All you see are tenants' names and codes. I don't know why that is. It's some security thing. So you got a list of names and codes. You dial the code, it rings the phone, you get a machine or a person, that's how you get inside. But if you don't know what code goes to what apartment number, you can't know what code to dial. Because, obviously, we don't have names either. I don't know the names of anybody in the designated households. My job is basically to find that out. Are you following this?"

I was.

"So what you have to do in a case like this is get inside and look at mailboxes so you can connect a name to the apartment you need to enumerate and then from the name get the code and then dial the code, hope a real person answers and that you can talk your way inside ... This is a real bitch of a process, especially when most people don't even answer their phones anymore until they hear who's on the other end and we are forbidden to leave messages. Anyway ... Jeff had done the footwork on this. He had gotten into the building and checked the mailboxes. From the apartment numbers on the boxes he got names. All I had to do was look up the names on the directory board outside and get the codes. Then I could dial up. So far, so good.

"Tuesday night, I got to the building at about 9. I must have been outside at that board for half an hour trying to get through to somebody. No answer. Machines, no people. The concierge came out and scolded me for tying up the switchboard. I tried one last code. It was Lamont's. He answered the phone and before I could introduce myself or anything, he said, 'Come on up,' and buzzed me in. I figured he was expecting somebody and he was going to be real disappointed when he saw I wasn't whoever he was expecting. But he wasn't. He was very nice. Cordial. We did the enumeration. He was too old for the study. We talked for a little while. Then, since I was inside the building, I tried a few more doors, just knocking, you know. I talked to a few people. Then I left the building at about 10, 10:30. But what I'm thinking now is that maybe whoever killed him saw me leaving as he was coming in. Maybe he thinks I saw him. Maybe he thinks I had been with Lamont and Lamont told me who was coming to visit him later on. Maybe he thinks I'm going to tell the cops."

I kept staring up at those dark windows on the top floor of the building. Lamont's windows. It was too creepy for me, all of it. Creepy and weird. And there was something off kilter about how Sean was thinking about it, too. Something irrational.

"So he goes to see you, to confront you? To see if you recognize him? To scare you? That doesn't seem real smart to me. Anyway, if you were going to tell the cops, wouldn't you have done it already?"

"You'd think. But since no one's come to bust him yet, maybe he thinks I haven't."

"But you might, so he wants to scare you."

"Scare me. At least."

"So say you find him and talk to him. What are you going to say? I didn't see you . . ."

"Right. Right, I say, Hey, man, I never saw you in that building the night you killed Lamont. And he says, Oh, that's cool. OK. Fine. Sorry to bother you . . ."

I drank some beer and thought how weird the whole thing was.

"I don't think that can be it, Sean," I said, stating the obvious. "He knows your name. The only way he could know that was if you'd interviewed him, right?"

"He doesn't sound like anybody I interviewed. He could have asked someone I interviewed for my name. Or he could have seen me on the street and followed me home. Then the rest is easy. Look at the name on the mailbox. Ask the neighbors. I get information from neighbors all the time. Names, work schedules, girlfriends or boyfriends, car the guy drives, what he does for work. You'd be amazed what people will tell you."

I opened my second bottle. Sean was on his fourth by now. We were out of beer.

"What a fucking mess," I said, suddenly getting the full gestalt in one big bang.

"Oh, you'd be so surprised the things they tell you," he said, still on that track. "See that window underneath Lamont's? I know who lives there. I know his name, his age, his sexual preference and what he does for a living. I know he plays golf on Sunday mornings, that he just broke up with his boyfriend who he bought the condo with, that the boyfriend took the furniture and left him the condo. I know he dislikes dogs. I have never talked to this man. He's never home. I got all this from talking to other people. Now his lights are on. Gee, if I wasn't drunk I'd just go right over and dial his code."

Clearly it was time for me to take Mad Sean, the Lunatic Enumerator of Parnassus Street, home to bed.

CHAPTER 10

In the midst of all this sex, mayhem and paranoia, I had forgotten entirely about Jeff.

Evan hadn't.

He caught me coming out of the bathroom Monday morning at the ungodly hour of 7:15. I wasn't planning to stay up or even wake up. He threw a few sentences at me and I grunted and went back to bed.

And had a dream.

I was staring at a computer screen that had the entire solution to the murder of Jeff Taylor on it. In fact it looked like a headline and it said, Murder of Jeff Taylor Solved.

I was reading the words on the screen and I pushed one of the F keys to make the words bigger. But instead of doing that, the screen cleared. I kept pushing F1, to retrieve the deletion, but nothing happened. I was so horrified that I had lost the text and couldn't get it back that I started crying and woke up with tears on my face.

Sean was sleeping beside me. Sunshine coming in through the blinds left dappled bars of light playing over his rib cage and side, white sun-stripes on his hair and across his cheek. We were turning out to be good lovers for each other, not afraid to let go, take risks. I trusted him in bed, which is not always the case. Which is rarely the case, actually. I trusted him, and I think he trusted me. He didn't rush me, that was what I liked. He took his time, and that involved a certain amount of trust. Like he didn't have anything to prove, nobody was clocking him, he wasn't working from a script. Some men have it all choreographed and you have to get the steps right and keep the beat. Well, whatever. But Sean didn't go into a different mode when he was having sex. He stayed himself all the time, a lover and a friend, both at once. It was a compelling combination.

I studied him lying there in my bed, a man asleep, totally vulnerable, and I thought, Mother of God, help me, I am falling in love with him.

Then I thought, Idiot, you should have prayed to Aphrodite instead. Why assume this is going to be one of those dolorous love affairs?

Well, why assume anything else? So far they all have been.

Then I remembered Evan and what he had said, or what I thought he had said.

I thought he had said he'd talked to a cop about Jeff's death and they had used a stomach pump.

"So what is he saying? He OD'd or something?"

"Or was poisoned."

"*Poisoned*?" Sean had just gotten out of the shower. I was staring at his body like I wanted to remember it because I'd never see it again—I was in that stage—and I didn't really want to talk about Jeff or murder or anything. I didn't even know why I'd mentioned it.

"I don't know what he meant. I don't even know if I heard him right. I was asleep."

"Great," he said. "When does he get home?"

"Seven-ish, usually. What are you doing today?"

"Going in to pick up some cases. I'll probably get some of Jeff's. The ID numbers come off the enumeration folders, and they're in order according to the listing sheets. So if I can get his listing sheets and even one of his folders I'll be able to find that respondent tonight."

"Are you sure you want to do this?"

"More than ever. Why?"

"I'm just . . ." I didn't know what I was. I just sat down on the nearest chair and started to cry.

He pulled up a chair and sat across from me. "OK, Alexandra," he said in his most soothing voice, "tell me."

I felt like clutching at him. I knew he was going to leave me. I was terrified of him leaving me.

What was this, hormones?

I wiped my eyes. I was an adult woman. A strong, tough, independent adult woman, though one with a bruised heart.

"I'm afraid," I said.

"Me too. So we shouldn't do anything then? Because we're afraid?"

"Ask me what I'm afraid of."

"What are you afraid of?"

I'm afraid of falling in love with you, I thought. I'm afraid this is all happening between us because of Jeff, because we're both involved in that. I'm afraid you don't love me at all, that as soon as this is over you're going to leave me for a man. I'm afraid of those two men on the answering machine. That's the emotional quagmire that is my soul at the moment.

But sadly, though my body trusted him completely, my brain didn't trust him enough to say any of that.

"It's been an intense few days," he said, filling in the blanks for me.

"The simultaneous conjunction of lust and murder," I said.

"And not much sleep," and he smiled at me and I felt instantly better. "If it's any consolation, I'm scared shitless too."

"Can I go with you tonight?"

"If you're sure you want to. I'll have to work for a few hours first. I have two interviews scheduled. After that though."

"After that I'll meet you somewhere?"

"I'll call you. It'll be around 9. OK?"

"And I'll grill Evan," I said. "And bring you some dinner."

"Way cool," he said, and smiled his endearing, half-ironic and self-mocking, half-totally sincere smile. "Grilled Evan. I'll bring the wine."

No true confessions this morning. I kissed him, naked and slightly damp as he was, and let him go.

I was looking at the Sunday paper, the Employment

Opportunities as they so euphemistically call the want ads, when I heard someone fiddling with the lock on the front door. Brave woman that I am, I froze solid, except that my heart started beating so hard I thought it would knock me off my chair. I couldn't even reach for a paring knife. But my brain was on overdrive and I realized that of course he'd taken my IDs, he knew my address, he was coming right through my door, and I was a sitting duck, or sitting goose, more like it. Idiot! And just as I was about to rouse myself enough to grab a butcher knife from the drawer, the door swung open and Jake ambled in.

"Hey, Alex," he said cheerily. "Long time no see."

He'd worked dinner at Greens, gone to a party, stayed over in the East Bay, was home to change, pick up some designs and go visit a client in the Mission. I asked him if I could tag along.

I had to cancel all my credit cards too, which I should have done yesterday. What a space case. The conjunction of lust and murder can sure screw you up.

I like hanging with Jake. He's the most laid-back guy I've ever met. Nothing fazes him. He's always in a good mood. I think he has a very active fantasy life so what happens on the everyday plane of existence is just a lot of white noise to him. That's my guess anyway. He seems far too content to be living full-time in this bizarre postmodern age.

Hangin' with Jake, everything's on slow. We drove in his ancient orange VW bug to Haight Street, again, so he could buy some flannel shirts at the Good Will. I looked at Doc Marten's wannabes, but didn't buy anything. I didn't have any money, my ATM card was gone, my checking account by now was probably empty, my credit cards charged up to the limit—I was broke.

While Jake was going through the racks of plaid shirts, tuxedo jackets, and stylishly torn jeans, I checked out faces. Maybe Fuller was shopping today too. After all, he had my last fifty bucks, might as well spend it.

We had to stop at all the other resale stores on the block too—Jake is not an impulse buyer—and I kept my eyes open. I saw a lot of strange, weird, flipped-out people, but I didn't see Fuller.

It took Jake an hour and a half to decide to buy two flannel shirts and a pair of engineer boots. The boots took the longest. He had to try on about twenty pairs. Finally I said, Jake, buy the boots now or I'll scream.

His client lived on Bartlett off 24th Street. There's a nice, funky café on the corner of 24th and Mission and I figured I'd wait there for him, sit at a big wooden table, have a cigarette and a coffee, read the paper, relax. I was uptight on Haight, which I didn't realize until we drove away from it and I could feel my shoulders return to their normal position, away from my ears.

I walked in and went right to the counter in the rear to get my coffee and a scone. There were two people ahead of me. While I waited my turn, I glanced around. I used to live in this neighborhood and even though it's been four or five years now, I still run into people I know on the street around here. So I looked around the café for someone I knew. Habit.

And I saw someone.

Fuller was sitting by the front windows, facing into the café, staring right at me.

He got up and left.

I was suddenly so pissed off at him, so enraged, that I ran out of the café after him.

The weather had changed; it had been overcast and chilly

but now the wind was up, it had started to rain, a real downpour, something we're not quite used to anymore. People had umbrellas up, but I swear nobody in San Francisco has any idea how to keep an umbrella under control. I nearly got my eye taken out by a few of them, dodging through the foot traffic on 24th Street, running after Fuller.

Valencia. The wind and rain now was intense. I could hardly see across the street. Then I saw him, or someone anyway, walking rapidly down the other side of the street toward 23rd.

I stayed on my side of the street, jogging along, letting him stay about half a block ahead, but keeping my eye on him. He got stuck at the light on 20th, but I ducked into a doorway and so when he glanced back behind him and across the street, he didn't see me. He'd lost me. He could relax.

I shadowed him all along Valencia, past Mission Playground, the biggest open-air drug market in the neighborhood, across 18th Street, into the roughest section of the Mission, between 18th and Market, east of Guerrero. I made the mistake of getting off BART at 16th and Mission one night around 9, and I thought I had died and gone to one of the circles of Dante's hell, the dim streetlights only barely illuminating the drugged or drunken men on the sidewalks, some half naked, some lying in their own piss on the ground, others in doorways, some still on their feet, stumbling around, looking insane, fighting with each other, out of control.

Sean had enumerated in this neighborhood too.

We were almost at 16th Street. There was a huge fruit market on one corner, the Roxie movie theatre across the street from it, a number of bodegas and shops, everything now drowning in sheets of wind-driven rain.

He crossed 16th and turned west toward Guerrero. I

ran across Valencia and up 16th to the Roxie. He was directly across the street from me—or he had been. Had he gone into the fruit store? Where the fuck was he?

A passing bus nearly drowned me, but I had to get closer, I had to see . . .

A hand grabbed me from behind, pulled me backwards.

I jerked away, trying to turn, rain in my eyes, rain pouring down my back now that my shirt was pulled away from my body, the shirt someone was holding tight in his hand, a tall broad Hispanic man in drenched jeans cradling a pineapple in his left arm who released his hold on me just as a truck the size of Angel Island came roaring through the very space where I had an instant before been standing peering out into the rain.

"Watch out, *chica*!" he said, releasing my shirt and smiling down at me. "Is too dangerous to cross here. Safer for you at the corner."

His smile was kindly, but he wasn't about to let me cross the street. No gringa suicides on 16th today, *por favor*.

I crossed at the corner, dutifully, after thanking him for saving my ass. Dumb broad. Run over by a truck. Jesus.

On the other side of 16th, I peered into the fruit store, didn't see Fuller, didn't really want to go inside to check. My brush with the Mack truck back on the street had shaken me and I didn't really feel like running into any more dangerous, moving objects. But, presto!, there he was, just standing there on the street not ten feet away, talking to another lowlife type, latino this time, in front of the building just next door. I ducked back behind the papayas and watched. A packet was passed from hand to hand, some cash. Right there on the street, in plain view, like don't even bother going into a doorway. Then the Latino went east, right past me, and Fuller turned into the building next door.

I eased out behind the stand of papayas and peaked around the bananas. Was he going to smoke it right there? But he was gone, disappeared. There was only one place he could be.

I stepped into the doorway; it was an apartment house. I checked the bells. No names on any of them. The mailboxes were inside the door and of course the door was locked.

"You look for somebody?" a voice said in my ear. I swung around to face an old Chinese man who had just materialized behind me with a dripping umbrella and a ring of keys.

"Yeah," I said. "But I don't know which bell . . ."

"I am building manager. Ask me. I tell you."

"His name is Fuller," I said, testing that theory anyway.

"Fuller? Nobody here named Fuller. Sorry. Wrong building."

"He's young. Real short hair. Tattoos on both his arms . . ."

"Oh, yes. I know. He visits friend in building. In number 317. Third row over, second from bottom. But bell not working. I let you in, OK?"

I thought about going into the building in search of Fuller—for about one second. My close encounter with that Mack truck struck me as a form of cosmic warning. I know when to quit.

"No, thank you," I said, smiling at him as as sweetly as I could manage with cold water cascading down my face. "I probably should call first. Thanks anyway."

He looked me over carefully. "My advice: go someplace warm. Get dry," he said.

CHAPTER 11

The Roxie was showing a film about Armistead Maupin, one of my favorite writers, a real romantic guy, so I felt safe standing under the Roxie awning. Sometimes they show strange and bizarre movies, and you can pick up the vibe of something like that. Sex and violence, murder, madness, sado-masochism—a brief window into my life, currently. Fortunately I had my camera in my pack, so I pulled it out and made myself look busy snapping rainy street scenes. This way they'd think I was an artist instead of a hooker. These small distinctions are sometimes very important.

I was hoping Fuller or whoever he was would come out of the building before I got pneumonia.

Thirty minutes later, he did.

He didn't bother checking the street. He was oblivious. He strolled west on 16th toward the Castro. I followed discreetly behind him.

The wind was intense, especially once we hit Dolores Park. On the avenue, the palm trees were bending and swaying, the rain was coming down in sheets, like we were in a tropical hurricane instead of a simple winter rainstorm.

Fuller walked with his head down, but I had to keep my eyes on him so I got the full blast of the wind and rain right in my face. Good thing I was looking though. He got as far as the corner of 18th and Sanchez, made a sharp left and went into the second store front. I waited a minute and then strolled by it. It was a gallery space. Queer Nation posters tacked up on the door, queer art on the walls. A drape hanging in a doorway between the gallery and what was probably some back room. Fuller nowhere to be seen.

I was ready to give it up. I was soaked, I was cold, I was feeling totally stupid, and ready for hot tea and a hot bath. I turned back to 18th and started home. Half a block down they swept right by me, without even looking, Fuller and two other punked-out queers. I picked up a little speed and followed along.

I was half a block behind them, between Hartford and Castro, when they disappeared into a bar. One of those boys-only joints with the black curtain over the door and the covered windows. Not my sort of place, but it is a free country after all. What were they going to do, throw me out?

Possibly. The vibe inside was not cool, not one bit. I was the only woman and I was scared for a minute until I remembered they were gay men and not dangerous. They only looked that way. It was all dress-up, all that leather hanging out at the bar so early in the afternoon. Then I remembered Lamont. I was about to turn around and leave on my own when a big leatherman, the bouncer by the evil look on his face, started approaching me and I thought, If he tells me to leave I'm going to raise hell . . . This is a public accommodation, blah, blah . . .

"Looking for someone?" he said, like that was the only possible reason a woman would be in a place like this.

"Yeah. Three guys who just came in."

"Not in here," he said. "Nobody's come in for half an hour." I almost accused him of being a lying son of a bitch, but I didn't because gay or not he scared the shit out of me. I'd just been thrown out of a bar. A famous first.

The good thing was that in the two minutes I was inside the rain had stopped. I took my camera out of my bag and felt it for water damage. I took the lens cap off and pointed it around, just to feel like I was a person again. Standing practically on my own street, certainly in my own neighborhood, just having been bounced from . . .

They were in my view finder. They were sitting at a table in the little coffee house next door. They weren't in the bar at all. They were drinking cappuccinos.

It was pretty dark but I opened my lens and slowed my speed and took a few photos. Then, because I was clearly invisible now, they didn't even look at women in this neighborhood, and Fuller especially didn't seem to know me from Adam, I went inside, sat at a table within earshot, and ordered a coffee.

Listening in on a conversation about people you don't know can be one of the most boring experiences. I had a book in my bag and so I pretended to read it. Fuller, the only one who might recognize me, had his back to me, so I felt pretty safe, sipping coffee, reading my book and taking notes on their conversation in the margins with my trusty pilot razor point. But the book was far more interesting than they were.

Until they started talking about Lamont.

Lamont's boyfriends.

Lamont's stuff.

The police.

Jeff Taylor.

"Bren was saying this shit Thursday night, before we even knew Jeff was dead. The shit's gonna hit the fan, he said. Well, it fucking did. Now I say we cooperate with the cops. Lamont's dead. His shit's gone. Somebody's got it . . ." This was the blond with the nose-ring.

"Doesn't mean whoever has it now killed him. A week's a long time." Fuller.

"Start where you start. Start with the shit. A Pentax K 1000. Seventy millimeter zoom."

"K 1000s are a dime a dozen."

"Just one minute." This was the third man, dark-haired,

with the gaunt, sunken look of a PWA. Like Fuller, he had an HIV+ tattoo on his forearm. "What you're saying is, we help them, they help us. OK, we help them. That much I get. But they help us? They're protecting the people who are fucking with us. They're paid by the people who are fucking with us. They *are* the people . . ."

"And one of them is among us," Fuller said grimly, and I jumped, thinking he was going to turn around and grab me by the arm. We were only inches away from each other. But he didn't notice me. He never once even turned his head in my direction.

"Paranoia," said the blond with the nose-ring.

"No. One of them is inside. Maybe more than one. I'm looking. I'm checkin' it out."

"Oh, man", said nose-ring. "Get over it."

"Suck my dick, Charlie."

"Suck mine."

"Look," said the PWA, "it's possible that QN is infiltrated. It's possible. Probable. They're inside abortion rights, they're inside Act-Up. We got spies in their organizations too. Just collecting information. They do it. We do it . . ."

"But they do it officially. Don't you get it? They have us fucking wired."

"Oh, man," sighed the nose-ring.

"Fine. But I'm not sitting in the same room with that asshole Metzer and talking about *anything*. Not the fucking time of day. Metzer and that other creep he hangs with, Len the Celibate . . . So clean he squeaks. Makes you wonder a little, doesn't it?"

"Right, man. If they don't let you come in their mouths you think they're Christian spies."

"That's fucking right."

"You're fucking crazy."

They'd finished their cappuccinos by then and were

getting up to go. I leaned way over my book so all they'd see would be my very wet head. The dark gaunt PWA-type said, "Hey, look who's prowling the streets. Saint Leonard himself."

We all looked. Luckily they were standing a little in front of me and didn't notice how my head shot up, how I took a chance and snapped the Celibate's picture.

Fuller was right about one thing. Given the grim times in which we live, he did look way too healthy to be queer.

They split up on Castro and I didn't feel like following anybody anymore. I went right to a two-hour photo joint and handed over my roll to get processed. If I wasn't in a rush I'd have done it myself, but I use somebody else's darkroom and that involves too much interpersonal stuff for times of stress. I didn't want to visit; I just wanted my photos. You know how that goes.

By then Jake was home totally pissed at me for deeking him like that. At least with him in the house, I felt safe enough to get into a hot bath and relax. Fuller still gave me the creeps and I still expected him to come climbing through one of my windows. But I had a different view of him now than before. He had a brain at least. A paranoid brain, but then if I were dying in an epidemic caused by a virus no one could find a cure for, which may have escaped from a government lab, but which the last two presidents could barely bring themselves to mention in public, gee, I might be slightly paranoid myself.

I was still thinking about Fuller several hours later as I was walking down Castro Street to pick up my photographs. He was paranoid, yes. But then, when you come to think of it, someone had been following him all afternoon. Someone had been listening to his conversation. Someone had even taken pictures of him and his friends without his consent.

If an amateur like me could spy on him as easily as that, what could more organized, more professional spies do?

CHAPTER 12

Evan hadn't come home from work yet when Sean called me at 8:30. He sounded depressed, but I was beginning to realize that that was pretty much the way he always sounded.

"Did you get Jeff's cases?"

"Yeah," he said. "Some. A bunch of them are still missing, but I have all his listing sheets. You still want to do this?"

"Don't you?"

"Yeah. I do. That doesn't mean you have to."

"Where are you now?"

"In a phone booth on Divis. I'll swing around and pick you up. Ten minutes. Wait outside, OK? I'll never get a parking spot on your block. And don't forget the interview." And he hung up in my ear.

I adore romantic phone calls like that.

We drove up Market Street and pulled into a parking area at the intersection of Corbett. Sean had one more call to make up here, another building he could never get into, but he had to make one last try, and while he was doing it I could sit in the car and go through Jeff's yellow enumeration folders until I found the one that had the same ID number as the interview. Then we'd have the respondent's name, address and phone number and we could take it from there. If we couldn't find the matching ID number on one of the yellow folders, we could still find the address by checking the ID numbers on the listing sheets. We'd find him one way or the other.

Sean said he'd be five minutes, max.

I turned on the inside light and the radio and went through Jeff's folders. There seemed to be something really macabre about it: his precise handwriting on the folders, his little stick-on notes stuck on to some with his own comments, reminders. Things like, Never call after 7. Or, Crazy lady, first floor. Or, Bring flashlight.

I found the matching ID number pretty quickly. The address on the enumeration folder was on Sanchez and I guessed by the number that it was close to the corner of Liberty. Inside was the respondent's name: William Blake.

It was only when I read the name and felt totally bummed that I realized that I was expecting an easy out on this one, an easy and sensible explanation for everything. I was expecting the name on the folder to be Fuller.

Time crawled along and Sean didn't come back. That could only mean that he'd gotten into the building after all and was doing the enumeration. What dedication the man had. It blew me away.

He had left his own enumeration folders on the back seat.

I put Jeff's back there and picked up Sean's. Just to see.

I had looked through these once before, but I hadn't been looking for anything in particular. This time I was looking for something. It wasn't a rational thing, just a hunch. Just something.

I went through the cases until I found the bunch for Buena Vista Avenue. I opened each one of them and checked out the names inside. If Sean had enumerated a household, and there were men in the household under the age of forty, he would have written down their names and ages inside the folder. I was looking for one name in particular: Lamont Bliss.

I found Lamont's. They started enumerating with the oldest man in the household and so Lamont's name was first. Lamont Bliss, never married, age thirty-five. But there was a second name too. Tom. No surname. Tom, never married, age nineteen.

I turned the folder over to the back where there was a record of all the calls made to the household and a brief summary of what had occurred.

Sean had rung Lamont's bell many times over the past month, and gotten his answering machine. But on Monday—not Tuesday, Monday—January 18, Martin Luther King Day—at 2:30 in the afternoon, he had been buzzed in and had talked with Tom, who gave the household enumeration, including himself as a resident. Since he was eligible for the study, Sean had made his pitch and Tom had agreed to be interviewed the next day, Tuesday, at 9 P.M.

On Tuesday, January 19, Sean had arrived at the building at 9 P.M., but when he called up to Lamont's he got the answering machine. He tried again at 9:30 and at 10. At 10, he was buzzed up by Lamont. When he got to the door and asked for Tom, Lamont told him that Tom was a friend, but that he didn't live in the apartment. Lamont didn't know where he lived.

Odd.

Then on Wednesday, January 20th, Sean must have been in the building again, because there was a very cryptic note on Lamont's folder: 10:20 P.M. I was leaving building, and saw R going upstairs.

But Lamont Bliss had already been murdered by 10:20 P.M., January 20th. He had been murdered the night before.

I jumped half out of my skin as Sean opened the car door and slid into the driver's seat beside me.

"Any luck?" he asked.

We careened down Market, heading toward Liberty and Sanchez. It was already after ten, but we were only reconnoitering, heading toward the address on the enumeration folder, going to check out the manor and estate of Mr. William Blake.

"Oh Rose, thou are sick!" Sean intoned as we ran the light and veered from Market onto 18th. "The invisible worm that flies in the night, in the howling storm, has found out thy bed of crimson joy: and his dark secret love does thy life destroy."

"What's that?"

"William Blake," he said. "The *other* William Blake. Or how about: Love seeketh not Itself to please, nor for itself hath any care, but for another gives its ease, and builds a Heaven in Hell's despair. So sung a little Clod of Clay trodden with the cattle's feet, but a Pebble of the brook warbled out these metres meet: Love seeketh only Self to please, to bind another to Its delight, joys in another's loss of ease, and builds a Hell in Heaven's despite."

"Wow," I said. "Were you an English major or something . . . like that?"

"You mean, something lame like that? Yeah, I was. And William Blake . . . well, I like him a lot. I wonder if people ever think about what they name their children. Imagine, William Blake, London engraver, writing poems about the need to liberate sexual desire. Blink, two hundred years later, William Blake, San Francisco hustler, living in a state of constant liberated sexual desire. Progress? Or what?"

I had never heard him talk so much. I had never heard such cynicism in his voice either. Then, I was feeling pretty cynical too. He'd lied to me. More than once. And if he'd lie about something trivial like how often he'd visited Lamont's and who he'd talked to there, who knew what other things, much more important, he might also be lying about.

But then he had warned me, hadn't he? And I had said I would trust him. I just wasn't sure I still did.

"By the way," I said, "I saw that man again today. The one from your apartment."

"Where? Why didn't you tell me?"

"When was I going to tell you? I'm telling you now. I saw him on 24th Street and I followed him . . ."

"You *followed* him?"

"Yeah. To an apartment house at Valencia and 16th."

"So," he said, "we've got him."

"I was afraid to go in, though."

"Afraid? Alex, you were sane not to go in. You were sane and smart . . . Promise me you won't try to find this guy by yourself. Please. Really, I'm serious. I don't want anything to happen to anybody else—you in particular."

He pulled the car over in front of some driveway, which on 18th Street is the only place you can pull over, and he reached over to me and held me very tight. "Promise me," he said.

My heart went into major melt-down and I promised him. Promise him anything, my brain said. Then do what you want. *Love seeketh only Self to please, to bind another to Its delight . . .*

Thank you, Mr. William Blake.

We drove on, up to Liberty and Sanchez.

There were plenty of places to park up there, though all of them on steep inclines. We parked right across the street from William Blake's house, which was one of those adorable little stucco numbers on Sanchez with their panoramic views of the city. It was a block down the hill from Liberty, which you got to by climbing a set of stairs. From there it was another steep block up to the top of Liberty and the stairway down to Noe, that same stairway Jeff had fallen or been pushed down, or OD'd on, died on somehow or other, or at any rate the place where his body had been found. There were lights on in the Blake household and I could see someone moving around in the kitchen.

Sean sighed and started to open the door.

"What are you doing?" I asked him, only slightly horrified.

"Gonna knock on his door," he said. "What else?"

He might be a pathological liar, but the man had balls, I had to give him that.

"What are you going to say?" I asked, opening my door, too.

"Hold it," he said. "Where do you think you're going?"

"With you," I said.

"No you're not. You're driving the getaway car. You're staying right here."

"Wrong," I said. "Where you go, I go. We're in this together."

"Look, Alex," he said. "I'm going as an enumerator. I'm gonna knock on his door and give him a rap about the study. If you come, you'll blow it. You have to stay here. Just be cool, OK?"

"Don't eat anything," I said. "Don't drink anything. Remember what Evan said."

He scowled at me and then he smiled. "Persephone in

the underworld," he said, like this was supposed to mean something, and got out of the car.

I watched him cross the street, go up the stoop, ring the bell.

My heart started pounding. I was so scared for him. I don't know what I expected, but nothing happened. The door didn't open. Not a crack.

"He's in there," Sean said, when he slid back onto the seat next to me. "He's definitely in there. I heard him. But he's also definitely not answering his door. Where's the nearest phone?"

"There's that market on 20th and Castro," I said.

"Right. I'll go and call. I think you should stay here in the car and watch the house. See if he leaves or if anybody comes. But stay here, OK? Don't go after him. Promise me, OK?"

"I'm cool," I said. "Don't trip."

He copied down the phone number from the enumeration folder and took off toward the stairs at the corner on 20th and Sanchez.

I stuck my head out the window and called him back to the car. "Wait a minute!" I said. "Where did Jeff live?"

"On Collingwood, across from the playground."

"Collingwood and 19th?"

"Yeah. Why?"

"Because if he was going home from here, he wouldn't go up to Liberty, would he? He'd go the way you're going, or he'd take the stairs at the end of Sanchez down to 19th, wouldn't he? I mean, he wouldn't go back up the hill . . ."

"But he wasn't on foot, remember? He had his car parked down on Church."

"Well, if he had his car parked on Church, why was he walking in the opposite direction down the steps to Noe?"

"I don't know, Alex," he said. "Let me go make this call."

Idle speculation was clearly not one of Sean's fortes.

But it was one of mine.

I sat in the car and watched the house for five, ten minutes. Then I got bored.

I guess I am basically an amoral person. I have no compunctions about breaking and entering and I have a real problem taking orders from men.

I got out of the car and walked up to the corner, crossed the street and walked back down the other side so that I would pass William Blake's house from the other direction. There was a garden beside his house, but there were motion lights on that side of the building so that wouldn't work, not at night anyway. On the other side of the house was the yard of the neighboring house, but there were probably motion lights pointed in that direction too. The only approach seemed to be a direct one: the front door.

I wondered if he'd come out if I just sat on his stoop and screamed. Or spray painted it. Or broke his windows. Or . . .

His front window was open. Melissa Etheridge was singing inside. A big orange cat was coming out.

His cat.

I could run over his cat. That might bring him out.

The cat jumped down and started rubbing himself against me the way spoiled cats do, expecting their allotment of affection, never expecting to get kicked in the ribs.

I tend to like people with spoiled, affectionate animals.

I sat down on the stoop and petted the cat. I was still sitting there when the front door behind me opened and someone coming out, blind or distracted, practically tripped right over me.

"Hi," I said, staring as doe-eyed as possible up at him with his very own cat lying voluptuously in my lap. "Sorry. I'm just into this thing with your cat."

"Oh," he said, a little miffed. "Well, playtime is over. He's got to come in now. Can I have him please?"

"Sure," I said, standing up but keeping the cat in my arms. "Where would you like him?"

He opened the door and said, "Give him to me." In the light spilling out from inside the house I got my first good look at William Blake, slim and reddish blond like his cat, and as adorable as his house, but nervous, I thought, a little high-strung, definitely on the hysterical side of the temperament spectrum.

I was playing for time now, holding onto the cat who was really quite comfortable in my arms and purring in ecstasy.

"Do you hear that?" I asked him, holding the cat closer. "He's a loud one."

"I really have to go," he said. "Do you mind?"

I did, I needed more time, dammit . . . and then, thank God, the goddam phone finally rang.

"Go ahead," I said to him, nodding into the house. "I'll let the cat in."

He was very ambivalent, but I sort of nudged him along, back inside toward his phone, stroking the kitty's neck as I did it, trying to look as innocent as a lamb.

Hah.

He picked up the receiver, watching me like a hawk, but then the voice on the other end grabbed his full attention.

"Wait," he said into the phone, "I can't deal with this shit now. I don't want to talk to . . ."

I shut the door behind me . . .

" . . . Not with the study? He's dead, you mean. I read about it in the paper . . ."

. . . and put the cat down.

" . . . How do you know he was coming here? . . ."

And smiled as sweetly as I could. Good old Sean had William Blake by the short hairs.

"William," I said. "tell him to come over. We all need to talk."

"Who the fuck are you?"

"I'm a private detective working for Jeff Taylor's family," I said, telling one of the biggest outright lies of my life. "You're in deep shit, you know. Tell Sean to come over and we'll all try to work it out."

Poor William. His eyes filled up, he was going to cry. "This can't be happening," he said, and then he started to sob. I get totally freaked out when people cry in front of me. I took the phone out of his hand and said, "Sean, just get your ass over here fast," and hung up in his ear.

See, I thought, I can be romantic on a telephone too.

I asked if he wanted me to make some tea or something. He said he'd rather hit the vodka in the freezer. Stolichnaya. I also noticed he had very expensive champagne in his refrigerator, very expensive scotch on his counter, very expensive flowers on his table. The gifts, I supposed, the in-kind payments, the bribes.

Ice cold Stoli with a twist in a Waterford crystal goblet. Jesus.

I introduced myself, figuring it was the only polite thing to do, since I was drinking his vodka, and asked him whether he liked to be called William. He said he preferred Billy. I said I preferred Alex. Sean was Sean. We were sorry to have to bother him. We were sorry about the whole business. But we had to find out what happened to Jeff Taylor and we hoped he could tell us. Then I asked him if the police had spoken to him—yet.

I think it was that that put the fear of God into him. Because it wasn't me, and it certainly wasn't Sean, who might be an enumerator from hell, but looked, even to my straight female eyes, like a dark angel, a Da Vinci angel, a Michelangelo angel. Billy the Kid Blake just about fell in a heap at his feet.

We spent an hour with William Blake. He admitted that he had spoken with Jeff several times during the days before he died. He admitted that he wanted some parts of his interview changed. He even admitted making an appointment to see Jeff on the night he was killed. But he denied, up and down and absolutely, that he had kept that appointment. Something had come up.

And I was one hundred per cent sure he was lying.

What was it about the interview that he needed to change?

He had revealed too much personal information, he said. He had talked about his childhood. He had mentioned a priest. He didn't want anybody to know about that stuff. He didn't want the government getting its hands on it. That was too personal, he said. He didn't mind the questions. It was all the other stuff, the stuff he had just said that Jeff had written down, that he wanted erased.

Then he decided not to bother after all and went out Thursday night instead of meeting Jeff. But he wasn't a complete jerk. He left Jeff a note, tacked on his door, telling him not to bother, everything was cool about the interview after all.

He said he was horrified when he read in the paper that Jeff had been killed.

He said the last time he had seen Jeff was the night

of the interview. They had met only those two times: the enumeration, and a week later, the interview.

He said he had no idea at all who would want to hurt someone as dear as Jeff Taylor.

Bullshit.

"You want to know what I think?" I said, finally running out of patience for polite discourse. "I think Jeff got your note, but that he came by again around 11 o'clock, saw your light on and knocked, and you let him in. I think you asked him for the interview and he tried to explain why he couldn't give it back to you. Then I think you put something in a drink and gave it to him so he'd get groggy and then you followed him to the stairway and pushed him down it and stole his pack. You didn't want to kill him but you did. That's what I think and I bet that's what the cops are gonna think too after we go and tell them what we know."

Sean looked at me horrified, like I had turned into some Gorgon right in front of his eyes, and I knew he was going to say that was nuts, the whole idea was nuts, because by then Billy had ingratiated himself to the point of actual seduction . . . but before he could blow it like that, Billy Blake, the lamb, reacted.

Or should I say, overreacted.

He stood up like he was about to go somewhere fast, took two steps forward, turned a sickening greenish white, tottered, and keeled over.

Everything in the entire house made of glass clinked and jingled like we were having an earthquake. He went down that hard. He was out cold.

Of course when someone passes out on you like that, you get soft and maternal. Unless there's some man around who's willing to get strong and paternal and take charge, in a paternalistic sort of way. Which Sean did, naturally, making sure I realized this was all my fault and I'd go to hell for it. Blah blah.

After Billy came to again, in Sean's arms of course . . . nicely orchestrated, Billy, I'll say that much for you . . . and got himself settled on the couch and began to look like he was alive again, and after I apologized and said that I might have exaggerated a little . . . and after he magnanimously forgave me . . . all this and Stoli too . . . he said two coherent things.

One was that he had been at the Queer Nation meeting on Thursday night and had been seen by thirty people at least, and then had gone out with friends, and didn't get home until after 2. So Billy Blake had himself an alibi.

Then he added, gratuitously, "Anyway, it was a mugging, wasn't it? It didn't have anything to do with my interview."

My interview, he said. Accent on *my*.

"Why did you make an appointment with him and then go to a meeting?" I asked. "If you were so keen on getting the interview changed."

"I just changed my mind about the interview," he said. "I stopped caring. That happens, you know. You can care a lot about something, and then, all of a sudden, you stop caring . . . Sean, could you be a prince and hand me a cigarette from that case by the phone?"

"You didn't happen to say anything to anybody else about the interview, did you? I mean, about your concerns . . . whatever they were?" It was an awkward question, but what could I do? I couldn't let on I knew what was in the interview. I couldn't say, Did you tell any of those closet cases that you named them? Did you happen to tell the General that you mentioned his name? Or the Very Famous Actor? Or Father Daly, Billy? Did you happen to mention it to him?

"What if I did?" Billy said, totally recovered now,

lighting his cigarette from the match Prince Sean had chivalrously lit for him. "I don't have to be confidential about my own interview, do I?"

Sassy brat.

"No. But maybe something you said might have concerned someone else . . ."

"Alex," Sean interrupted. He was getting uptight now. It was his ass on the line after all. Jeff might have been killed over this, but, jeez, Sean could get fired! "Let's go now."

But I kept my eyes on Billy's face and I thought I saw something, a sort of twitch, like a brain cell somewhere was hitting itself on the head and going, Duh! He went real pale again.

He had talked to someone.

Sean was pushing me toward the door. I turned to Billy and said, "Hey, if you think of anything . . ."

"We'll get back in touch with you," Sean said as he pushed me out the door so hard I tripped on the steps and nearly fell and broke my neck.

"You're a fucking rude son of a bitch," I said to him as he pushed me across the street toward the car. "We might have been getting somewhere."

He waited until I was in the car and had my seat belt on and he had started the engine and shifted into gear. Then he said, "Two things, Alex. One, the first thing he said to me was that he knew Jeff was dead because he read it in the newspaper. But he never read that Jeff was killed in the newspaper because they didn't mention his name in the newspaper. And two, Billy's datebook was underneath his cigarette case. *Voilà!*"

"Oh my God," I said, as Sean produced the book from under his shirt.

"So I thought we should just haul ass out of there."

What a hell of a prince. A prince of thieves.

CHAPTER 13

"I can't believe you stole this," I said, holding Billy Blake's leather datebook in my hand. "Don't you think he'll miss it?"

"Not tonight. He has a date later and by tomorrow we'll have returned it."

"We will?"

"Yeah," he said. "I also took his back door key . . . I used to be a JD," he added, grinding the car to a halt at the corner of 18th and Castro and smiling angelically over at me.

"A JD? Is that the Eugene equivalent of a Blood or a Crip?" Sean was from a little town outside Eugene, Oregon, otherwise known as Granola Central.

"A juvey, hun. A juvenile delinquent. A bad boy. A burglar . . . I was real good at breaking and entering. I just never found anything I wanted enough to take. Before this. So we'll read it and return it tonight and he'll never know it was gone."

"Why are you so into this?" I asked, keeping my eyes on the men crossing the street in front of us, the old leather queens, the young politically correct queers, the hustlers. Everything out in the open on the street, and still I never knew who was who or what was really going on. Even living here, even having gay friends, I still felt totally outside this culture, never getting the signals straight. Well, none of the signals were aimed in my direction anyway, so why should I even think I should get them?

Why should I care if I knew what was going on or not? I could be living in Chinatown; then I wouldn't even understand the signs in the shop windows. I mean, it could be worse.

"Into . . .?"

"This," I said. "Finding out about Jeff. Why are you so into it?"

"Why are you?"

"Because . . ." I still had my eye on the street. I was hoping to see something there. I don't know what. Something that made sense to me. " . . . because . . . I'm tagging along with you, that's why."

"Oh," he said. "Cool."

The light changed and we drove on, crawling along in search of the ever more elusive parking spot. I guess we were going to my house to check out the loot.

"Well? You didn't answer my question."

"Why I'm into this? Because I liked Jeff, I guess. I liked him a lot."

"That's the only reason?"

"Isn't that enough of a reason?"

"But what if Billy did kill him, Sean? I mean, what if he actually killed him?"

"He didn't."

"But how do you know? He went there Thursday night, he was poisoned, he was thrown down the stairs . . . Somebody did it."

"I don't think he did see Billy Thursday night. I don't think Billy had anything to do with it—overtly. But he knows something. That's obvious."

"Why don't you think he went back Thursday night?"

"Because he was with me."

"Until 10:30, you said."

"Did I?"

"Yes. You said 10:30."

"God, what a memory you have."

"Well? What do you mean he was with you? What do you mean?" I was beginning to sound a tad hysterical.

Which he caught, of course. "Chill, Alex," he said. "I wasn't fucking him or anything. Jesus."

"Well? What do you mean then?"

"I mean I was with him. In his presence. We were together, see? In a bar. Drinking."

"Why didn't you tell me that then?"

"I don't know," he said. "Sorry."

"So, then what happened?"

"I dropped him off at his car on Church at about 11:30. Then I drove around the corner to a market and called you. They found his body at midnight. He didn't have time to go see anyone. He either was killed right there on Church and dumped at Noe, like you said. Or he walked up the block, maybe on his way to Billy's, but he never got there. There just wasn't time, Alex, see? There just wasn't time . . . Besides, Billy has an alibi, remember? He was at a meeting, then he was with friends . . ."

"What else haven't you told me?" I asked him.

"A lot, Alex. I'm sorry. I warned you."

"Were you and Jeff lovers? . . . Just tell me that one thing. Please."

Bad timing. He caught sight of a parking spot just at that moment and pulled into it. Perpendicular parking on a very steep hill—my favorite. I had to push with all my strength just to get the door open. He had to push with a lot of his to get his door closed. That's how we cross-train in the City: walking up and down hills and opening and closing car doors at forty-five degree angles.

Then we were standing on the street together and then we were walking and he could, of course, pretend he hadn't heard the question.

"Well?" I said, feeling gorgonesque again, my personal forte these days.

"No," he said. "We were friends . . . It is possible, you

know. To love someone without fucking him. I know it's very out of fashion at the moment, not to fuck everything that appeals to you. It's very retro. Well, Jeff was a retro kind of guy. That's one of the things I liked about him. And he was hitched to this complete idiot . . ."

"I thought you liked Brendan."

"I said that too? Jesus. Yeah, well, I liked Brendan all right. In bed. But as a human being . . . So here's another possibility for you, Alex. It's possible to love someone you'll never have sex with, and have sex with someone you'll never for one second love. How's that for a mind fuck, huh? So much for romance in our time."

We walked along the street for awhile with this cold silence between us. Then he moved a little closer and put his hands on my shoulders and turned me around to face him.

"I'm sorry," he said. "But you wanted motivation, right? Well, that's it. I fucked his boyfriend and I feel guilty about it. OK?"

I said sure, fine, OK. I felt like crying again but I held it in. Swallowed it. It's not like I wasn't expecting this, after all. It's not like it came as some kind of major surprise.

But he put his arms around me and said, "I should have told you before. I'm really sorry."

"So," I said, remembering the wording of the survey question on sexual identity, "which of the following terms best describes how you think of yourself: heterosexual, straight, homosexual, gay, queer, bisexual, other?" And then I did sob, right on his shoulder and much too loudly. I was mortified. I didn't want him to think I was some kind of wuss who couldn't deal with a little thing like this, and deal with it heroically, manfully, etc. Who would go all weepy and weird on him. Who would act like a bimbo.

"Alex," he whispered right in my ear, "can we talk about this someplace else?"

We went to my house. Evan was there. Jake was there. Friends of theirs were there. Party time.

Sean stashed his case of blood samples from the day's interviews in our refrigerator and grabbed a couple of beers. We slipped into my room and before I knew it we had slipped out of our clothes and into my bed and into each other and I felt so much better, which I guess was his point, like there are certain things you don't talk about any place but in bed and only after many long intense orgasms so you're in the right frame of mind to hear it.

"Don't go to sleep," I said. "We have the datebook, remember?"

"I'm not going to sleep," he said. But he was.

"Sean, I want you to tell me now. Don't go to sleep. Tell me."

"About what?"

God, he was so dense.

"About Jeff and Brendan . . . About you and Brendan. Please tell me."

We were lying next to each other, both of us staring up at the ceiling. Evan, or maybe it was Jake, was playing some Miles Davis. Nice and mellow. I really wanted another beer, but I'd live.

"There's nothing much to tell you about me and Brendan. I met him one night when I went out with Jeff. About a week later he called me and asked me to meet them at a bar. When I got there he was alone, made up some story about Jeff working or some shit . . . Turns out Jeff didn't know anything about this, of course. He wasn't even in town that night. We wound up in bed. His place. His idea. This was about a month ago, I guess. Before

Christmas. I haven't seen him since, and I would be happy if I never saw him again, Alex, and that's the truth.

"Thursday night I ran into Jeff, like I told you. I didn't know if he knew. I didn't know what their arrangement was, you know. We went to a bar. We talked about work. He told me about the problem with this interview. But, see, I wasn't really listening, not closely, you know, because I was so hung up on whether he knew about me and Brendan, and if he did, what he was going to say. Finally, he started talking about Brendan. I knew right away that he didn't know we'd had sex, which was a relief. He knew Brendan was fucking around, though. He went on this whole thing about how you couldn't trust a gay man, how in his whole life he had never known one gay man he could trust. With his heart, you know. Faithfulness, that's what he wanted and he couldn't find it with anybody. He went on about that, about how fucked up it was, everybody lying, nobody trustworthy . . . Well, I felt like shit. Here he is talking to me about trust and I'd just fucked him over. And I couldn't tell him. Then he laid this bomb on me. Brendan had just tested positive. Just that week. Jeff was devastated, Alex. It was like the world had ended. Sure he knew Brendan was screwing around, he knew that. Brendan was too politically correct to be faithful. A charter member of Queer Nation. Gay sexuality is free, lusty, promiscuous. Celebrate your sexuality, fuck in the bushes. Choose death—Brendan was full of all that shit. Sexual fidelity as a heterosexual plot. Gay men don't break each other's hearts, gay men don't link sex and love. Blah blah. Well, Jeff wasn't buying it. His heart was good and broken—and he was raving mad. I mean raving. He went on about gay men going around merrily infecting each other with a fatal disease, but how nobody in the community had the balls to say anything about it. Like who exactly is infecting us? Who's doing it, exactly? The whole rhetoric of how nothing should stand in the way of the perfect orgasm, not even the threat of death, not even murder. That's what he kept saying: people were fucking murdering each other and excusing it by saying that we're all responsible for ourselves, we're all equally culpable. And I just felt so helpless, Alex. I mean, what could I say to him? He was so in love and he felt so betrayed. He could have lived with knowing Brendan was screwing around. But he couldn't live with Brendan being positive. He couldn't live with that. With that level of stupidity. Of carelessness. Of Brendan's just not loving him enough to stay alive for him. That's how he saw it. It was a really intense few hours we spent together. And then next thing, minutes later, Alex, he's dead. Thirty minutes later. Less. So, see, I have to find out what happened to him. I have to find out who killed him, even if what I find out is that he killed himself. He'd do it for me. I know he would."

I didn't want to introduce the banal and mundane into this hymn to male bonding, but I was basically a pragmatic sort so I waited a polite thirty seconds and then I asked him if he was planning to get tested again, now that he knew about Brendan.

"No. I just was tested, a few months ago. I can't stand doing it more than twice a year. I'm real, real careful. But how careful can you be? . . . How about you?"

"I was negative last time I checked."

"Yeah, well we're all negative last time we checked. Except when we're not. Sero-conversion, we call it in the trade. Who knows how long it takes to sero-convert, huh? Two weeks? Two months? Two years? We don't know shit about this virus . . . We're all gonna die anyway, Alex. Look at Jeff. He was negative, but he's dead too."

"Would he have killed himself?"

"I don't know. I hope not. Jesus, I hope not. But we'll have to ask Evan about that stomach pump business."

He was awake again at least, which was encouraging. We had a long night ahead of us, going through the datebook, and getting it back inside Billy's house. Talking to Evan. Maybe at some point getting some sleep.

I got up and started getting dressed. I didn't want to say anything heavy or stupid to him. I wanted to be cool about everything because cool is the spirit of our times, after all. I thought he was a pretty romantic person himself, and so he would have his own ideas about what was going on between us, if anything, and when the time came he would say something. The word love, for example, which had never yet been spoken between us except in reference to other people.

"I love watching you get dressed," he said. "Almost as much as I love watching you get undressed."

"I love that about you too," I said. And thought, Well, the "L" word . . . what progress!

"By the way, I never answered your question."

"Which one?"

"Which of the following best describes . . ."

"Never mind, Sean. It's none of my business . . ."

"I think it's your business. We're lovers now, aren't we? You have a right to know."

I sat down hard on the bed with a big black Converse basketball sneaker in my hand. A really big one. Too big to be mine.

"When did we go from being whatever we were before to being lovers?"

"Just now," he said. "All you have to do is say it, and that's what it is."

"Oh," I said. "Like God naming the animals?"

"Did God name the animals? I thought Adam named the animals."

"Well, whatever. You're naming us, I guess."

"Is that OK? Do you mind? Want to call us something else? Good friends? Sexual partners? Uh... fuck buddies?"

I kissed him very hard on the mouth. "Lovers is fine with me, Adam."

"Good. And in terms of sexual identity, though I must say I'm drawn to the polymorphously perverse 'other' category, which I guess means you do it with animals and furniture and tree trunks and inflatables, I'd say I'm bi on the cusp of straight."

"Bi on the cusp of straight," I repeated.

"And getting straighter by the second, Alexandra."

He said my name like he was saying "I love you". So I said it for him. "I love you," I said.

"You're so brave," he said. "I love you too."

CHAPTER 14

It was another hour before we emerged from my bedroom. By then everybody else was sound asleep.

We got beers out of the refrigerator and sat down at the kitchen table with Billy's datebook.

His datebook was like a doctor's appointment book, divided by hour. Most of his evening hours were accounted for. Hour by hour, he had a very active social life.

"What are we looking for, exactly?" I asked, paging through the month of January. The man wasn't hard up for dates, that's for sure, but he made his notations in code: first names or initials. No overt assignations with

Governor Wilson or General Colin Powell, but I guess that would be too much to ask. "When did Jeff interview him again?"

"On the 14th. Is it there?"

I looked at the 14th. A Thursday. Small note at 9 P.M.: "AIDS interview." Sandwiched in between "Ted" at 7 and "MD" at 11:30. He was booked up Friday night. Ted again, at 7. A regular. He was out of town on the weekend, in Monterey. Where he had a slew of appointments.

"Monterey," I said. "Army base."

"Hmm," Sean hummed. "Beaches, too. Don't get fixated."

"I'm not fixated. It's January. Nobody goes to the beach in . . . Oops," I said. I had turned the page from Saturday the 16th to yesterday, Sunday, the 24th. Pages must have stuck together, but then I was snagged. He had made a big black cross over Sunday. Like the day had been erased, and over it, in big black letters: TED.

I flipped back to the previous week, the week of Sunday the 17th. Ted, every night at 7. Back through the week of January 10th, and there it was. January 13th: "Ted/hospice" and the phone number. It was the hospice Evan worked at. I knew the number by heart.

"Ted must have died yesterday," I said.

"Huh?" Sean said. "What are you talking about?"

"He went to see him every night at the hospice. He died yesterday."

"Well, we picked a shitty day to hassle him then. Sorry, Bill."

"What are we looking for again?"

"We want to see if Billy had a date with anybody he might have named in the interview between the 14th and the night Jeff was killed. If that's possible."

"It's not. It's all initials and first names. I mean, how could you tell who 'Bob' is? It could be Robert Redford."

"Sure," he said. "It could be Bob Dole."

"But, wait," I said. "How many Jeffs could there be?"

"What?"

"Well, here, on the 18th, at 3 P.M. 'Jeff. Dolores Park.' And, wait, on the 19th. Again at 3 P.M. 'Jeff, tennis court'."

"They were meeting in the park? That doesn't sound like Jeff."

"At 3 P.M.? That doesn't sound like Billy."

"But they were meeting. So he lied to us. He said he only saw Jeff twice, and clearly he didn't."

"If this is the same Jeff."

"Is there a Jeff before the 14th?"

I looked through the month as quickly as I could. Page after page of little notations every hour or so starting at about 7 P.M., with Ted. He must have gotten his beauty rest during the day. Or he had a day job. But then those two 3 P.M. meetings, erupting into his afternoons like monoliths in the desert, like those huge standing rocks in Monument Valley.

"No Jeff before the 14th," I said.

"Huh. And what about after the 14th . . . What about correspondences with those names in the interview?"

"Well, who exactly?"

Sean went through the interview, naming names. I copied them down on a piece of paper. Then we compared names with Billy's datebook notations.

Eureka! But eureka a bunch of times. There are, after all, only so many letters in the alphabet, and there was no way to determine whether the initials in the datebook corresponded with the initials of the very famous actor or homophobic general or the state legislator or anybody for that matter. Of the thirty-five men Billy Blake had named, most were probably regular, normal gay men with regular normal lives. Stockbrokers, lawyers, school teachers, men with names like Mike and Todd, Lyman and Leslie, Stephen, James and Marcus. Who could tell which of these men might have been severely inconvenienced by public exposure, in addition to the Flight Commander, the General, the Honorable State Legislator, the Very Famous Actor? Who were we to figure this out?

"This is really impossible," I said.

"But he did talk to Jeff. On the 18th and the 19th. They must have met to talk about the interview. But why not meet at his house? Why in the park?"

"Because Billy was paranoid and scared and freaked out. That's what Jeff told you, remember?" I said, thinking about slow-acting poisons. "He needed that interview back. Then all of a sudden, he didn't care about it anymore. Odd."

"We'd better return this book," Sean sighed. "I'll go get the car."

"We could walk," I said. "It's nice out. And I don't get out much this time of night."

"And you know why that is? Because only lunatics, drunks and predators come out at 3 A.M. We have enough trouble in our lives right now. We're driving."

Funny, he should say that just then. At that point, 3 A.M., Tuesday, January 26th, we still didn't know what trouble was.

It seemed to take forever for him to get back with the car. It was on dead empty; he'd had to drive all the way to Divisidero to get gas.

We parked on Liberty, up by the stairway, and walked down to Sanchez.

In my humble opinion, it's one of the best spots in San Francisco. Looking west, you see the rolling hills of the Castro and the lights of Sutro Tower up on Twin Peaks. Looking north, you see the lights of downtown, and east the lights of the Mission. Lights in all directions, spread at your feet. The whole brilliant city at your feet, and still you are surrounded by trees, flowers, pretty little houses, so you feel like you're in the city but not of it, floating above it somehow, immune to its sorrows.

We walked holding hands, breathing in the scent of jasmine, moved, both of us, I think, by the stars above us and the lights below, and just a tad terrified, or I was, of breaking into William Blake's pretty little house.

There was not a single soul on the street.

We took the stairs at the corner of Liberty and Sanchez and walked down the block to Billy's house.

A light was on upstairs.

Billy's cat was crying at the front door.

"Watch the motion lights," I whispered, as Sean opened the side gate to the garden.

"So the lights go on. We have a key."

"But what if he's home?"

"If he's home, we get caught. But he's not home yet."

"He might be. His cat's out."

"Jesus," he said. "You would notice the cat."

We walked through the garden. The motion lights went on, as I knew they would. I started shaking, but maybe it was because it was chilly out. We got to the back door and Sean tried the key. I was about to say that it was probably dead-bolted from inside, but it wasn't, it opened up, like magic, and there we were, in Billy's kitchen, switching on the light.

And there was Billy, strung up spreadeagle across the living room doorway, tape over his eyes and mouth, his whole body cut open, blood everywhere, all his insides hanging out.

CHAPTER 15

I took in the sight of slaughter, blood and ripped flesh, a man's intestines spilling out onto the linoleum, an instant of it, and then I was being gentled back out into the garden. The motion lights were still on. The lights of the city were still twinkling below us like earthbound stars. The crescent moon was still up in the sky.

I sat down on the ground and waited for my blood to stop pounding in my veins. As soon as I could, I reached over to touch Sean who was squatting next to me. He had that sickly greenish pallor Billy had had earlier. Then, thankfully, the motion lights switched off and we were in darkness again.

"This can't be happening," he said.

Billy Blake's words. The hair really stood up on the back of my neck then.

"It's happened again," he said. "The same way."

I concentrated on breathing.

"I can't deal with this," he said. "It's out of control."

"Sean," I said, totally overcome by the instinct to flee. "Let's go now."

"It's the same, Alex. The same as Lamont. The same tape on his eyes and his mouth. Did you see? The same cuts. The same way he's hung up there. It's exactly the same."

"How can you know that?" I asked him, feeling that creeping sensation up my back again.

"I saw him," he said. "I have to go back inside for a minute. I just have to see . . ."

"Sean! Wait!"

We both stood up. The kitchen door creaked open. I thought I was going to die on the spot.

"The cat," he said. And then he took a step forward and puked in the bushes.

I was crying, but I knew we had to go, fast. But Sean wiped his mouth on his arm and turned back toward the door. "You can't go back in there. Sean, please."

"I have to look one more time," he said. "Wait for me."

I waited. I couldn't even move.

I heard him talking inside. Who was he talking to?

"Fuck!" I heard, and then the light in the kitchen went out and he reappeared next to me, and threw something into the bushes.

"Fucking cat," he said.

We got as far as the stairs.

Two men were sitting on them, making out.

We walked up the street. The car seemed miles away. When we climbed up to it finally and got in, I noticed that Sean's right arm was bleeding. The cat had scratched him, two long, deep cuts.

I took his arm and kissed it and then I licked the blood, remembering the way Evan and I would lick each other's scratches when we were kids. He pulled his arm away. "Are you crazy?" he said.

That did it. Everything broke open. I didn't think I could cry like that, like when you're a kid and you cry like it's the end of the world. You don't care. You just let yourself go because it's all too much.

It was all too much.

And I loved him too much.

He held me and let me cry all over him. He held me and I loved him so much that I knew if he died, I'd die. If he had it, I'd want it too. If he was going to die of AIDS, then I would die of AIDS. I didn't care.

"We have to be smart about this," he said.

I was blowing my nose. We were driving home. It was 4:20 A.M.

"Do you think we should call the cops?" I asked him.

"I thought it was against your religion."

"It is. But we can't just leave him . . ."

"Right. So we call the cops. Twice in one week."

"We didn't call them last time."

"I called them. For Lamont."

"You called them?"

"I found him, just like we found Billy."

"Why didn't you tell me?" I was getting used to these little surprises, but this one really floored me. "You never told me . . ."

"I couldn't tell you. I promised someone . . . OK. This is what happened. I had a respondent. Some guy living in Lamont's apartment. On Tuesday I went to interview him and Lamont told me he didn't live there. Well, it happens. People break up. One day they live there, next day they don't. But if we make contact like that and the respondent moves, we can still do the interview—if we can find them. So on Wednesday I was back in the building enumerating and I saw this guy, who supposedly didn't live there, going upstairs. So I followed him up. I needed to ask him where he was living, so I could do the interview. I got to Lamont's and the door was open, so I went in. And found him."

"What happened to the other guy?"

"He was there too. Barfing."

"Oh."

"He was totally out of control. He flipped right out on me. I called the cops from a pay phone and then I took him to my place."

"Who was he?"

"Some really young kid named Tom. Said he was nine-teen, but I didn't believe him. More like sixteen . . . Street kid. Runaway. Terrified of the cops. Terrified of prison. Terrified of being sent home. One of those kids who's been fucked over since he was born. Lamont was the only good thing that ever happened to him. Brendan happened to him, too, which was not a good thing. We had that experience in common ... Tom was the reason Jeff wouldn't finish the building. He knew Tom was living with Lamont. He also knew Tom and Brendan had slept together and he couldn't deal with doing an interview with him, asking him questions about what kind of sex he'd had with his own lover. I mean, that makes sense, right? Jeff liked Lamont, but he wasn't in love with him or anything. It wasn't Lamont he didn't want to see. I sort of lied to you about that. I'd sworn to Tom that I wouldn't mention seeing him that night, and I didn't know you well enough to tell you back then. Last week. Whenever."

"No wonder you were such a wreck when you came to see us on Thursday."

"Yeah. I'd just dealt with this kid all day. Who was totally ready to move right from Lamont's bed into mine. Very needy kid. Very very easy lay. For anyone interested." He glanced over at me. "I wasn't. The kid has real bad karma. Real real bad."

"What happened to him?"

"No idea. I gave him some money ..."

"He doesn't have an HIV positive tattoo on his left arm, does he?"

"I don't know, Alex. Like I said, I made him keep his clothes on."

I turned on all the lights in my house and while Sean made coffee I woke up Evan. We needed real sanity, and I wasn't anything like sane anymore.

The first thing Evan did was go out and make the call

for us. He wouldn't call from the house, since they had call trace on 911. We wouldn't want the cops showing up at our door looking for the San Francisco Ripper. We had enough trouble without cops all over us too.

Sean had left fingerprints at two murder sites. He had Billy's back door key on him somewhere, and Billy's datebook, and Billy's cat had his blood all over one of his claws. He'd be in serious shit if the cops got hold of him.

"Somebody's killing gay men in this town," he said to Evan when we were all sitting around the table drinking black coffee and smoking cigarettes. "Two, maybe three in one week. That we know of. How many more . . ."

"Three in one week? We lost four at the hospice this week. That's seven. One a day. And I knew six out of seven. Jeff's the only one I didn't know."

Evan rubbed his face, stifled a yawn. He looked really tired, rumpled and sort of a wreck. We looked across the table at each other, and we must have looked pretty much the same, male and female version of tired, rumpled and sort of a wreck.

"I'm really sorry about Billy," Evan said. "I liked him. I liked Ted, too. I really liked Ted. He was funny. Outrageous, even when he was dying. He made us laugh on his fucking deathbed. I liked him best of everybody. He was my man, you know how you latch on . . . you keep hoping. Don't take this one, that kind of hope. Not him, God, OK? Just let him . . . He was so cheerful at the end. He was so happy. He said that outing that right-wing bastard was the best thing. Miss Robert Rightwing, he called him. He was so tickled by that . . ."

"*Outing him?* Outing him?"

"Yeah. What?"

"He wasn't outed, Evan. He just came out. By himself. How do you know he was outed?"

"Ted told me. But everybody knew it, Zand. It wasn't a secret or anything."

"Ted died yesterday?"

"Yesterday. Sunday. I don't even know what day it is. Why?"

"And it was a natural death, right?"

They both looked at me like I was nuts. "Yeah," Evan said. "Real natural. Total organ failure. Multiple internal lesions. He bled out. Age twenty-three. If that's a natural death . . ."

"I mean, he wasn't murdered, was he?"

"He was. In a manner of speaking."

"Never mind," I said. "I'm going to bed."

"Wait, Alex," Sean said, catching my arm. "What are you getting at?"

I stood in the kitchen with my fists in my eye sockets trying to remember what I'd been getting at before Evan went all Act-Up and political on me. I couldn't remember anything. My mind was a total hole. Not even a blank: an abyss.

"I can't put the pieces together," I said. "But there's Billy and his interview. And Ted knowing that right-wing asshole was going to be outed. And Jeff dead. And now Billy killed . . ."

"Go to bed now," my brother said looking as paternal as a twenty-nine year old in sweats can look at 5 in the morning. "Tomorrow is another day, Miss Scarlett, Mr. Rhett. And tomorrow you're going to have to think real seriously about talking to the police."

"About what?" Sean said. "All we'll accomplish is getting ourselves into a big hassle."

"You might get into a much bigger hassle . . . Well, look. Let's talk about this tomorrow. After you get some sleep."

"But you won't be here," I said.

"I will," he said. "I need a mental health day. And now, beddy-bye. Are you sleeping with my sister, Sean, or would you like a bed of your own?"

"Oh," Sean said, "thanks, Evan, but Alex and I are mates. We'll share. By the way, Alex said you mentioned something about Jeff and a stomach pump. What was that about?"

"I ran into a cop I know. He told me Jeff had been killed with a stomach pump."

"What!" Sean said, like the image alone made him feel crazy. It made me feel crazy, anyway. "How could he . . ."

"It's a gun," Evan said. "A small .22. Very small. Fits in your hand. Can't be seen. It's made for real nasty street fights. You're in a fist fight, see. You go to punch a guy in the stomach, but you got this little .22 in your hand. He can't see it, he thinks you're just punching him. But when you make contact with his stomach, you pull the trigger. You're so close, you have the barrel up against his body, so when you fire, there's no noise. You don't hear it. It sounds like a punch. Bullet goes right in. Can't miss. You can fire two, three times . . ."

"Somebody shot him," Sean said, like he couldn't believe what he was hearing and had to repeat it to himself. "He didn't kill himself. He was murdered."

"And whoever killed him had to be real close," Evan said. "They know that from the powder burns."

"So it wasn't suicide," Sean said. He sounded utterly relieved. I'd never considered how the idea of Jeff's committing suicide might have been affecting him. And he'd never said anything. But I guess if you have an intense talk with someone and then ten minutes later they kill themselves . . .

"No, it wasn't suicide," Evan said. "Not unless he shot himself in the stomach a couple of times and then managed to hide the gun."

"Listen," Sean said. "Whoever killed Jeff, killed Billy Blake. He killed them for that fucking interview."

We all knew it, of course, but hearing it made me start to shake.

"I'm going to find that fucker," Sean said. "I swear to God I am."

CHAPTER 16

It was early in the morning, about 9, when Evan shook me awake and motioned me to be quiet and come with him. Sean was sleeping with his arm over me, so it was hard to disengage, besides which I didn't really want to. I had been blissfully asleep and now I was miserably awake and it was grey and raining outside on top of it all.

"What?" I snapped at him in my most nasty, how-dare-you-wake-me-up-so-early fashion. He shut my bedroom door and handed me a cup of coffee.

"We have to talk," he said.

What he meant was that he had to talk. And this is basically what he said: you stumbled on a dead man; you have to tell the cops; you still have the interview that the University probably reported stolen, so you have, really, stolen property in your possession; and anyway who is this guy you're sleeping with and what do you know about him besides the fact that all these dead people had had some contact with him just prior to their sudden exits from this plane of existence?

"He's from Oregon," I said. "And he's a Leo."

"Zand," my brother said, and he looked so serious and

so *brotherly*, "will you please just answer me and not joke? Please?"

"OK. Sure."

"You found a dead man today, right?"

"Right."

"And you said, *you* said, he was killed the same way Lamont was. Didn't you? In fact what you said exactly was, 'Sean says he was killed the same way Lamont was.' Right? Now what did you mean by that?"

"Sean found Lamont's body. And he said it was the same. Masking tape over his eyes and over his mouth, his body cut open . . . It was really horrible, Evan."

"I'm sure it was. Really, really horrible. Are you OK?"

"Now I am, yeah. I didn't even puke. Sean did."

"Now, did I hear you right? You just said, Sean found Lamont's body. Is that what you said?"

"Yes, Evan. That's what I said."

"Do you see where I'm going with this?"

"No, where are you going?"

"He says he was the last person to see Jeff alive. He found Lamont's body. He found Billy's body . . ."

"Oh, OK. I see now. Wherever Sean goes, Death follows. He should start wearing garlic or . . ."

"Alexandra."

"Look, no, I don't see. I love him, Evan. OK? I love him. He didn't kill anybody. If that's what you're thinking, even remotely . . . get over it."

"You love him?"

"Yes."

"Zand, I want you to listen to this. Don't get real upset, OK? But you have to know about this."

He rewound our tape and pressed PLAY.

"Al-ex-an-dra. Slut of Persia," It was—surprise! a male voice. "I'm looking for Brendan Maddox's fuck buddy, Sean the Enumerator. Is he there? Yes? No? Well tell him this for me, Al-ex-an-dra. I have a message for him from beyond the grave and I would like to deliver it before it gets all rotty and stinky on me. *Esta muy importante, puta*, you got me? Tell him to be at the bench on Kite Hill at dusk tomorrow, Tuesday, or the message gets dumped from my disk, got it? And tell him if he comes looking good and hard I might just sit on him."

I knew that voice.

"Well?"

"Maybe Sean knows who it is. I don't."

"Well, I don't either, but I sure as fucking hell don't like coming home to shit like this on our machine, Zand."

"I'm sorry," I said. I felt like I'd been hit twice, once by the voice on the tape, once by my own brother. I started to get up to go to the bathroom, but he caught hold of my arm.

"Come here," he said, and he hugged me tight, which was just what I needed to start bawling again. "I'm sorry. I didn't mean to come down on you like that. I'm just scared for you. I don't want you involved in this. I want you to talk to the cops. Please."

"Why are you thinking this about him, Evan? Why?"

"Brendan Maddox is a militant Queer Nation activist."

"So?"

"If this guy on the tape is right . . ."

"You're going to believe this asshole on the tape?"

"OK. But say it's true. Say, for the sake of argument, that Sean . . . OK, forget it. I'm sorry. Forget it. Just tell me you're being so careful, so intensely careful, I don't have to worry about you and him, right?" he said.

"That's not what you meant," I said. "That's not what you were going to say."

"That's a big part of it."

"What's the other part?"

"I read that interview. It's dynamite all right. If Queer

Nation could get hold of something like that, they could out a lot of fucking evil men in this state . . . and they'd do it, too. So maybe Sean . . ."

"Oh, I see. Maybe Sean killed Jeff for the interview that Jeff had already sent to him in the mail for safekeeping."

"Well, that's what he says."

"Why would he lie?"

The words were no sooner out of my mouth than all the lies Sean had told me came rushing into my head.

He had lied a lot.

Or at least withheld the truth. Which may or may not be the same thing.

He had told me he hated Brendan. But then there were those messages on his tape.

He had told me he loved Jeff. But then . . .

"And what about Lamont? You have a theory for Lamont too?"

"No. Not yet."

"Evan, please stop this. Please."

"All right. All right, I'll stop. But you know what would make me really happy?" Evan tried smiling at me while he wiped the tears off my face with his hand. "I know you're going to hate this, but just think about it, OK? I would like you to go to Elizabeth's for a few days. Don't tell him where you're going. Just go to Mill Valley, sit in the hot tub, drink all their Dominus wine, eat all their food . . ."

"I can't leave him," I said. "I can't, Evan."

"Then tell him you have to talk to the cops. And see how he reacts. Just see, Zand. If he flips out on you . . ."

"And what exactly will I tell the cops? We broke into Billy Blake's house to return a stolen datebook and found him hanging like a slab of meat from his doorjamb?"

"Yes. You tell them the truth. You give them the interview and you stop playing private eye. This is serious business, Zand. Somebody is killing people."

"Sean couldn't do that to anybody," I said, remembering Billy's body a little too vividly. I could almost feel myself turning green. "Besides he was with me . . ."

Except he wasn't the whole time. It had taken him nearly three-quarters of an hour to gas up the car.

CHAPTER 17

I didn't call the police. The police called me.

Or rather, the police came to my door, dripping wet.

A Detective George Kagehiro, Homicide, San Francisco Police. It was 11 A.M.

Detective Kagehiro caught me as I was coming out of the shower. Evan was still drinking coffee. Sean was still asleep.

Detective Kagehiro asked if I was who I was, apologized for disturbing me, and especially apologized for bringing me sorrowful news. He was so sorry to have to inform me that an acquaintance of mine by the name of William Blake had been murdered during the previous night. Would I possibly be able to help him in his investigation of this tragedy by answering one or two small questions for him?

I must have turned color because he said again that he was very sorry and was this a terribly bad time to come?

I said no so long as I could put some clothes on first. He said that was cool, or the cop equivalent, "No problem."

How the fuck did I overnight get to be a known acquaintance of Billy Blake?

I hoped that Evan would keep his mouth shut. I could throw on a pair of jeans in about half a minute, but Evan could talk fast, mellow as he is. And Jake was up and about, too, getting ready to go to Greens. And Jake could easily ask if Sean had spent the night. Jake is mellow but curious.

I checked Sean. He was sound asleep. I wanted him to stay that way. I wanted to gag him and tie him to the bed, but I thought that might be a bit extreme. But he needed to be warned, so he wouldn't come waltzing out in the middle of the interrogation. I woke him up enough to tell him to stay in bed. "Don't move until I tell you it's OK," I whispered to him. "We have bad company. Promise?"

He grunted and rolled over.

I wanted to roll over with him, but I pulled on a t-shirt instead and went out shaking in my boots to face the Man.

He was sitting at the table talking to Evan about the rain.

Thank you, God.

"I wonder if I might speak with your wife alone?" Detective Kagehiro said to Evan as I joined them at the kitchen table.

"Alexandra's my sister," Evan said. "And if it's all right with her . . ."

"Stay, Evan," I said, and so he did.

I sat down next to him and faced the detective. My heart was pounding, and it wasn't a caffeine rush though I had had too many cups of Evan's horrible black coffee. Evan slipped his hand under the table and squeezed my leg. Encouragement maybe or a signal that now was the time to spill my guts. Whatever.

Detective Kagehiro began by giving me a very brief and sanitized version of Billy's murder the previous night. Could I deal with a few questions right now? I nodded.

"Were you a close friend of the deceased?" Detective Kagehiro asked with great sympathy in his voice.

"No," I said.

"How well did you know him?"

"Not well," I said.

"Under what circumstances did you meet?"

I searched my brain for this one. Creative Responses, 101.

"Actually," I said, lunging at this furry image in my head, "I knew his cat."

"His cat?"

"Yes, I used to pet his cat whenever I walked by his house. We met that way. Just introduced ourselves on the stoop, that's all."

"I see," he said. "And did you pet his cat yesterday?"

"Yesterday? Yes, I think so."

"What time was that?"

"It was in the evening."

"Can you be more precise about the time?"

"Eight maybe?"

"Eight. All right. Well, thank you very much," he said and started to get up. "You didn't happen to make a date with him while you were talking to him at 8 o'clock, did you?"

"A date? No. Why?"

"He was writing you a note . . . Perhaps you'd like to see it?"

He took a piece of paper out of his attaché case and handed it to me. But before I could reach for it, Evan took it out of his hand so I had to read it over his shoulder. It had been a mistake, I guess, to introduce myself using my real name. Luckily I hadn't introduced Sean to him. Luckily I didn't have all the social graces down pat.

Neither, evidently, did my very rude brother.

The note, addressed to me, said, "After you left tonight, I did think of something else. Please come by Wednesday night, same time, after 10, I'll be here. I'm sorry for all the . . ."

It just stopped there.

"The phone directory was open to your page. You have an unusual surname. There's only one of you in the book."

"Evan's in the book," I said. "Not me."

"But he'd already addressed the envelope. He'd even put a stamp on it. He just never finished the note. But you see, it suggests you were there last night after 10. Which is 2 hours after 8."

I wanted to tell him I could add too.

"I'm sure it wasn't that late," I said, lying stoutly.

"And what could it mean, that he thought of something else?"

"We'd been discussing cats," I said. "How to get rid of fleas."

"I see," he said. "You also have a cat?"

"No," I said. "The fleas got too much for me."

"Well," he said. "That's all then. For the moment. Thank you for your time."

He took the note back from Evan and then let it drop onto the table almost directly in front of me. Evan picked it up and handed it over.

"Don't lose it," he said.

"Don't worry," said the detective. "We never lose evidence."

"God, what a sly bastard," Evan said after Detective Kagehiro went back out into the rain and I collapsed at the table in a heap of ragged nerves and fried brain cells. "Did you get what he was doing?"

"Trying to get me into Billy's house at 10 o'clock, yeah, I got it."

"No, Zand. He wanted you to touch that note. He wanted your fingerprints."

"That's illegal," I said, hoping it was.

"Sure it is. So is search and seizure. Tell it to Bill Rehnquist and the Supremes. I'm sure Antonin String-'em-Up-Without-an-Appeal Scalia would really object to the cops lifting your fingerprints off a piece of paper or coffee cup. I'm surprised he didn't snatch your cigarette butt."

Simultaneously we checked the ashtray. All butts duly accounted for.

"Was I OK?" I asked.

"You lied like a trouper."

"Sshh, he might be listening at the door!"

We checked the door too.

Detective Kagehiro wasn't there.

I went into the living room and stretched out on the floor. I was shaking so hard I thought it was the house. I got a rush of earthquake terror for a minute; then I realized the tremors were coming from me.

Evan came in too and lay down next to me.

"Did he believe me?" I asked him.

"No."

"Well, what the fuck does he think? I killed Lamont Bliss and then I killed Billy Blake the same way? What for? Why? I mean, do I look like a serial killer to you?"

"Not to me, no. But then who knows what a serial killer looks like?"

"Thanks," I said. "Well, it's all true, Evan. I tied him up, hung him from the doorjamb and slit him open. Singlehandedly."

"No, not singlehandedly. You had an accomplice."

"Of course I did. Sean and I and Billy were into a little three-way S and M scene, two S's and one M. The M got the shaft and the S's got to go home and sleep late."

"Relax, Zand. They don't think you killed anybody. They just think you may know something. Which, may I remind you, you do. They think you were in Billy's house last night. Which you were. Twice. Do you mind if I ask you why you lied to the nice detective about it? I mean, Zand, it's a murder investigation. I don't think it's wise to lie to . . ."

"I have to talk to Sean," I said.

"What about going to Elizabeth's?"

"No."

"Zand," my brother said, "you're a big girl now and everything, but will you at least consider the possibility that your boyfriend may be a very sick man?"

"I'll consider it," I said. "But not in Marin."

And that was that.

CHAPTER 18

I went into the bedroom and sat down on the bed next to my sleeping boyfriend to consider the possibility that he might be a very sick man.

He had lied to me, that was true.

He had warned me, though, that he was going to.

Was that a characteristic of a very sick man?

Besides lying to me, what else had he done? Discovered two dead bodies and stolen a datebook. Hardly characteristics of a sick man.

For a few minutes, I sat quite still on the bed and watched Sean sleep. I tried to think like Evan and imagine my lover beating Lamont Bliss to death, shooting Jeff Taylor with a stomach pump and slicing up Billy Blake. I couldn't do it.

But what did I know about sick men? Not a damn thing.

Finally, I woke Sean and told him about the tape and my encounter with the police.

If Evan were right, he'd react somehow.

He did. He kissed me and said I was the most wonderful being on the face of the earth.

I like that in a man.

Evan watched like a hawk while Sean listened to the message on the machine.

"I don't know who that is," he said. "But I'll meet him. Alone," he added looking at me. "You're not going."

"You're damn straight she's not going," said Evan.

"Well, fine," I said, letting them bask in their machismo. "I'll just stay home and bake bread. By the way, I have something to show you."

I dug around in my bag and retrieved the photos I had taken the day before. They had come out pretty well, considering the light problem: 16th Street, the building Fuller or whoever he was had gone into, a bunch of shots of the three pierced and tattooed Queer Nationals sipping cappuccino, the Celibate walking down 18th.

"This one," I said, pointing to the group photo. "He's the guy who broke into your apartment."

"I know that guy," Evan said. "He volunteers at the hospice."

"He does?" I said. "Really?"

"Yeah. Why not?"

"He's weird," I said. "What's his name?"

Evan just shrugged. "Don't know his name. He's good with our clients. What can I say?"

"And this one is Charlie Coyote," Sean said. "I've met him with Jeff and Brendan. The dark guy is Joseph Angelicus."

"OK. Who's this?" I flashed the photo of Len the Celibate.

"Never saw him before," Evan said.

"Me either," said Sean. "A little on the chub side, isn't he? He's gotta be straight."

"He's in Queer Nation," I said. "I don't think they let straights into Queer Nation. I think there's some kind of queer test they give you . . ."

They both stared at me.

Such humorless men.

Around noon, Evan got guilty about taking the day off and went to the hospice where he was always needed and so never had to feel like he was just sitting around wasting time with his freaked-out sister, who might be crazy but wasn't close to death yet. Sean said he had to go enumerate and interview. The show must go on. I said I needed to go back to sleep.

I opened the frig and and there was the plastic case filled with Sean's blood samples, little blotches of blood each in its own specimen case, labelled with ID number and date.

I got out the milk and had a bowl of Cheerios. It was about all I could stomach.

Evan kissed me good-bye and left to do good deeds at the hospice. Sean kissed me good-bye and left to do good deeds in the field, finding gay and bi men to pluck with a needle, a wicked thing in fairytales, but in this case forgiveable given all his good intentions. Myself, I kissed everything good-bye and left to do absolutely wicked deeds, namely to spy on my beloved, the enumerator.

Because I was in love with the man, but Evan had planted seeds of doubt and I hate seeds of doubt. I needed to know absolutely and for sure that the man I thought I loved was really the man I had in bed with me, that I wasn't blinded by love or sleep or karma, that my soul wasn't bullshitting me. I needed to know what he was up to.

The rain had stopped, the sun was out, it was getting warm. A great day for a walk and, lucky for me, Sean must have thought so too because he didn't take his car. He walked down 18th toward Upper Market. He stopped at a café and got a coffee to go. He stopped on the street and talked to a middle-aged man walking his poodle. This was a rather animated conversation, but I was too far away to hear anything. I couldn't let him see me. And he would. I wasn't invisible to Sean—at least I hoped I wasn't.

We were almost to Market Street before I realized where he was heading. He was going straight toward Kite Hill.

Kite Hill is one of those San Francisco open spaces, a mound of wild earth with paths and a few benches, set aside, one might guess from its name, in a more innocent time, for municipal kite flying, now more likely a place to get high. It was really a beautiful afternoon, a kite-flying sort of afternoon. Not that anyone was flying kites on Kite Hill.

I didn't go climbing up the hill. I watched Sean climb. Two homeless-looking men were sitting on one of the benches, playing a radio. They watched him climb the path like he was their next meal and I was momentarily afraid for him. Silly woman. He went right up to them and engaged them in conversation. He gave them cigarettes, which I suppose they asked for. They pointed to various spots on the hill, like they were giving him a geography lesson. That's when I got what he was asking them: what's the light like up here at night; where are the benches; who hangs out after dark; would they be here; how many packs of cigarettes would they want to watch his back.

I hid behind a bush as he came down. He walked practically right by me, heading up the street toward Market.

Market is a thoroughfare up there below Twin Peaks. Four lanes, all of them fast. But Sean wasn't crossing Market, not here anyway. He was walking up, back toward the building he had enumerated the night before. Before we went to Billy's. Before all that.

He crossed Market at Corbett. He wasn't going into the same building after all, but one quite like it, very plush, very modern, great views. Did he have an interview there?

The buzzer at the gate was still on when I got to it and I slipped through. I slipped through the front door too, and noted the floor the elevator was stopping at. I ran up the stairs and got to the third floor in time to see Sean go into one of the apartments. Apartment 305. I put my ear right to the door, but I didn't hear a thing.

Next step: check the mailboxes.

I was heading down the hall on my way to do just that when a man got off the elevator and passed me. I walked very slowly so I wouldn't get to the stairs before I saw what apartment he went into. As soon as the door shut behind him I ran back down to check. It was apartment 305.

The man was Joseph Angelicus.

San Francisco is a small city inside of which the Castro is a small town. People tend to know each other; social circles overlap. It was certainly possible that Sean was enumerating in an apartment whose owner was a friend of Joseph Angelicus. But that might be stretching coincidence a bit too far.

And it was. The names on apartment 305's mailbox were Angelicus and Stone.

I waited outside until Sean emerged, about twenty minutes later, far too short a time to complete a gay/bi interview, that much I knew for certain.

He walked back down Market, this time as far as 19th. He turned up 19th, climbed the stairs. Up there on Corbett were more of those new buildings clinging onto the side of the granite face of Twin Peaks, the greatest views at the highest prices and in buildings that looked like the tiniest shock wave would send them tumbling down like a bunch of tinker toys. Evan assures me that clinging to granite is the safest place to be in an earthquake, but it's not the sort of real estate I'm interested in, thanks anyway.

Sean strolled down Corbett until he got to a very pretentious-looking building, all windows and façades and fancy flower gardens in front, fancy cars in back. The neighborhood, creeping up both sides of Twin Peaks, was becoming the gay version of Pacific Heights. This apartment building in particular had so many gates it made you dizzy just thinking about the security system. It made you wonder what they were protecting so vigorously. It made you want to break in and see.

Sean picked up the intercom phone and waited. He

dialed again. Someone must have answered because I could see him talking into the phone. He took out a cigarette and lit it and talked more intensely into the receiver. This wasn't an interview either.

He hung up and smoked his cigarette down to the filter. I was hiding again, behind another bush. Anybody watching out his window would probably think I was stalking Sean, or a mugger about to spring. Anything but what I was, just a snoopy, suspicious woman with a camera trailing her lover around the city. The camera helps though. If nothing else, it gives me something to hide behind. And it keeps me amused. I take pictures of cats in windows and nobody suspects I'm staring in the window with a telephoto lens.

Within a few minutes, the gate opened and a very young, very skinny, very tattooed punk kid emerged from the building. They stood apart from each other for about thirty seconds and then the kid threw his arms around Sean and held him tight.

They went inside. I went home.

I needed a woman to talk to, but all my women friends lived out of town, in Taos or Santa Fe or Portland or Seattle. We had all fled the Bay Area at the same time, between the Oakland fires and the L.A. riots. Coincidence, I guess. And I couldn't very well call them long distance in the middle of the day when the rates were so high and lay this on them. For one thing, in the middle of the day, very few productive members of society are at home.

Still I was wishing for a warm female voice to talk to over the telephone when, like some bad cosmic joke, my sister Elizabeth called.

"I'm in town Friday," she said. "Same time, same place? I assume you haven't found a job."

"I'm working on it," I said.

"Well, the St. Francis then? It's so *convenient*."

Not to me it wasn't, but then Elizabeth as usual was referring to herself.

"I can't believe you're coming in to shop again, Elizabeth. Doesn't he keep you on any kind of budget?"

"No, he doesn't. But I'm not shopping, as a matter of fact. I'm going to the museum in the afternoon and then Jeremy and I are attending a fundraiser in the evening. So I can slip you in between Jeff Koons and Lyman Jasper."

"Gee, a perfect fit," I said, wondering how much dough Jeremy would be dropping into the coffers of the Republican Party this time. Jeremy, to whom I never referred if I was in a conscious state, was Elizabeth's rich, right-wing husband who had made his money in munitions and so believed the military was God, since it had provided very well indeed for him, and after all, that's what counts. "How's Jeremy taking the lifting of the ban on gays in the military, by the way?"

"A complete boondoggle," she said. "Clinton's supposed to do it tomorrow. Just like that! Can you believe it?"

"Yes," I said. "It sounds very presidential."

"Jeremy says he'll never get away with it. He says the military won't let him. We'll see who really runs the country, Alexandra, and it's not the faggots ... or Bill Clinton."

"I hope you were still quoting your husband on that one, Elizabeth. I mean, I hope you're not calling gay men faggots now, under his nefarious influence."

"Nefarious, Alex? Really. Jeremy is a thoughtful, loving, responsible ..."

"Asshole. *But* you're married to him, so of course he's wonderful. A wonderful asshole. Look, I don't really care about gays in the military at the moment, but if I can I will meet you at the bar on Friday. Just don't bring Mr. Wonderful with you, OK?"

"No, he'll be meeting with Jasper. Personally. Jeremy says Jasper has the tightest, best financed, most sophisticated political organization in this state and they're completely dedicated to . . ."

"Elizabeth," I said, "they're a bunch of Christian fundamentalists. Remember those abortions you had? Remember all those men you 'fornicated with' before marriage? Remember wild sex, free love, LSD? Don't you get it? They think you're a sinner. They'd like to stone you, Elizabeth. Get a life, will you?"

"As usual, Alexandra, you're completely exaggerating. Being a fiscal conservative and believing in family values and moral living does not make a person . . ."

"Read *Handmaid's Tale*," I said, gruffly. I just couldn't listen to her barfing out that shit anymore. "For God's sakes, it's bad enough you married a Republican, but do you have to turn into a gender traitor on top of it?"

And I hung up in her ear.

That's it, I said. Go to Marin? I'd die first.

CHAPTER 19

I didn't like being home alone. I didn't want to think about Sean. I didn't want to remember Billy's body. I wanted to be somewhere else, in another reality altogether. I was glancing idly at the movie listings in the paper when the phone rang again and I jumped half-way across the room.

The man on the line wanted to speak to Sean.

"He's not here," I said. "Can I take a message?"

"Yeah," the man said. "Tell him Brendan called about the car."

"That's it?"

"Can you take a longer message?"

No, Brendan, I'm brain dead. But what I said as sweetly as I could was, "Try me."

"He asked me about some stuff he left in Jeff's car. Tell him the car was parked right down the block but somebody broke into it over the weekend and, you know, took shit. So I don't know what he left in there, but chances are whatever it was, it's not there anymore."

"Is the car still there so he could check?"

"It's either there or in our driveway. A friend was going to get it towed. Window's broken. Door's broken. I mean, he can check. Everybody else in the city has.

"Also could you tell him I'm sorry we keep missing each other. Tell him I had to come here . . . I'm home, in Michigan . . . for the wake and the funeral and everything. But I'll be back Thursday. The memorial service is Thursday at 7. Tell him I'll call when I get in, but if we don't connect, maybe I'll see him then."

I said I'd tell him all that. I was about to say that I was sorry about Jeff, but he hung up before I could get it out.

How strange, I thought. Would anyone in his right mind, about to bury his lover, make a call like that? To tell somebody about a trashed car? But given the situation in Michigan, Brendan might not be in his right mind. Anyway, the call probably wasn't about the car at all. It was about Brendan and Sean. It was the call you make from a funeral parlor to the one person whose voice you need to hear, maybe because he's the person you really love.

I needed to get out of the house and away from the phone in case somebody else I didn't want to talk to decided to call. I was out of cigarettes anyway so I headed toward Castro Street.

As usual, there was a pedestrian traffic jam at the corner of Castro and 18th. It was one of those magnetic corners where gay men gathered in droves, waiting for the bus, waiting for the traffic light, waiting for Prince Charming, while other gay men leafletted them about Queer Nation demos, the next Mr. Leatherman contest, or the newest Cambodian take-out joint.

I loitered on the corner for a minute or two, just looking around for a familiar face. Looking for Sean, actually, not that I really expected to see him there.

It appeared that this afternoon Queer Nation was working the corner, getting signatures on a petition and handing out flyers. I took a flyer from a guy in a bomber jacket weighed down with enough rainbow flag and pink triangle pins to set off a metal detector.

"Rally tonight at Harvey Milk Plaza," he mumbled, obviously bored with the whole project, or else he'd been repeating the same lines out here for hours.

"What for?" I asked though I could read the reason in bold print on the page in front of me: *Queers murdered! Cops ticket jaywalkers!*

He didn't answer. I hate that level of distraction in a political zealot.

"Well?" I asked. Then I took a good look at him. All I'd really noticed before was the jacket, the pins, a pudgy stomach, turned out feet.

It was the man I'd photographed walking down 18th Street, the one the cappuccino drinkers referred to as Len the Celibate. He sure looked like a militant queer to me, though a bit on the nerdy, lackadaisical side.

"Well what?" he said, keeping his eyes fixed on the bus that was inching its way into the intersection.

"What's the rally for, exactly?"

"Oh," he sighed. "More cops in the Castro. Neighborhood foot patrols. Protection."

"Well, good luck," I said as he meandered away from me to hand out flyers to a group of queer suits getting off the bus.

"There's a petition you could sign," he said over his shoulder, but the traffic light had changed and I made my escape.

I didn't think more foot patrols in the Castro was the answer to this particular problem. Anyway I'd never sign a petition to ask for more cops, serial killer or no serial killer. Cops and vampires: invite them in and you're asking for trouble.

Dusk was coming on and Sean wasn't home.

I wondered where he was, who he was with. Who that kid was who had thrown his arms around him on Corbett Street. Why he had gone to see Joseph Angelicus, how much he knew about the man with the tattoos who had come all over his bed. I wondered if anything he had told me was true.

I had known him less than a week. I had known Evan all my life. Evan would never hurt me, not for anything. Why didn't I trust his judgement on this one? Why didn't I listen to him and go to Marin?

Love seeketh only Self to please, I thought sadly.

That was probably why.

I dressed warmly and stuck a flashlight in my bag. A flashlight. What else did I need? I probably needed a gun, but I didn't have one. I wished I had gotten that tattoo. The bleeding heart of Jesus on my left bicep was what I really needed tonight. Or a big dog.

I walked down 18th and over to Caselli and there I was in the deepening twilight at the foot of Kite Hill.

I took one of the paths up. It was steep and I couldn't really see much. The moon would have been out except for the clouds. Still there was a pallor to the air, the suggestion of light.

Up on top was the bench where the homeless men had been sitting. No one was sitting there now. I kept walking along the path. There was another bench farther up; it looked empty too. But there were definitely presences on the hill, people in the shadows, in the recesses, the gullies. It felt as though hundreds of people were living in warrens among the grasses, under the dirt, behind the bushes. It felt like the hill was alive, but with ghosts, shades of the dead.

I was shaking. I had managed to scare the shit out of myself.

I got to the top of the hill and looked around. Homeless men were sitting together in depressions in the earth. An older person was walking a dog. Someone was standing alone looking out at the city, smoking. Was that person Sean? It was getting too dark to make out faces, to make out people, to tell the difference between a person and a shadow, a live man or a hungry ghost.

I stood at the top of the hill and I wanted to cry out his name and make him come to me.

Maybe I just wanted to cry.

I turned around and saw two men sitting close together on the bench I had passed on my way up. And one of them was certainly my lover.

"Well," I heard as I approached, "if it isn't the other half of the nice het couple. Turning into a breeder on us, Sean? I'm surprised at you! Or did Brendan scare you straight after all? He's a demanding little nellie Act Up bottom, isn't he?"

"Alex!" Sean said, getting up.

"Oh, Alex, is it? Nice to meet you. Again."

Sean practically jumped the guy. "Who the fuck are you, anyway?" he yelled. I'd never heard him so angry.

"I'm a little T-cell, short and stout. Here is my handle, here is my spout . . . No, Sean, dear, I'm just another one of Brendan Maddox's one-nighters. There was me, there was Tom, there was you, and about 200 others. Don't feel bad if he doesn't remember you though. Swallowing all that cock's done something to his brain. He just can't tell one dick from another anymore. But Jeff was another story, wasn't he? Jeff was the best. And for some bizarre reason that escapes me, my man, he cared enough about you to leave a message for you. With me. In case anything happened to him. Which it did."

"What message?"

"He sent you something in the mail. You still have it?"

"Why?"

"Because somebody wants it real bad. Don't tell anybody you have it. Dump it. Fast. End of FAX."

"Jeff told you about it?"

"Jeff told me everything. He knew, see. He had an eye for things. He had a gift."

"What else did he tell you?"

"He told me he wanted to kill me. Came to my place with a gun. Little faggot with a gun, what a joke. I said, Oh, please shoot me. Please do it, sweetheart. Blow me off the wheel. Want to see my lesions, honey? Go ahead, shoot me, save me some medical expenses. Save me a lot of trouble. Oh, Lord, yet more trouble! Remember that line? They were pulling the guy's guts out at the time. Those English and their ways! Jeff would have pulled mine out cheerfully. Blamed me for giving his lover the virus. Right, I said. Me and how many other armies? Don't be so ignorant, I said. Your boyfriend's the biggest slut in town. Like he didn't know. Well, turns out he didn't know. He was one of those very naive, very trusting people. So I said, You want revenge? You really want to kill somebody? I can give you a list, starting with George Bush and Jesse Helms and Pat Robertson, Falwell, Buchanan, the fucking Pope. You want to go out in a big way—take your fucking pick. Well, he didn't get to the Pope, but he did something. He did do something, though nobody's ever gonna know it."

"What did he do? *What did he do?*"

"You don't know? He outed Miss Robert Rightwing, Robert Slatley, only son of God's avenging angel. The bitch who says AIDS is God's judgement on homosexuals. Because we're such wicked sinners. Cause and effect. Sodom and Gomorrah, Part 2. Miss Robert's mom gets the Christians all fired up and sends them out to bash us. And little Miss Robert was her executive officer. Jeff had been told, in confidence of course, that Miss Robert was a frequent guest of a certain avowed homosexual— that is the expression they use, isn't it? *Avowed homosexual.* Has a rather noble, chivalric ring to it, doesn't it? So Jeff took the bull by the horns and outed Slatley. Or threatened to. He made the call. He could have kept making them too. He would have, but something got in his way. Doesn't matter. We're all gonna die from this thing one way or the other."

"So somebody killed him? That's what you're saying? Somebody who knew . . ."

"Look, man. A friend of mine disappeared on the corner of Market and 17th. Last seen, they said. Like he was a lost dog. Last seen on the corner of Market and 17th. And never fucking seen again. Then there's Lamont. Then there's Jeff. Then last night, Billy Blake. That's my reality, man. We get into cars and we're never fucking seen again. We get murdered in our own fucking houses.

We die in the fucking gutter. Jeff needed to die for something. He needed that. And he got it. But he doesn't want it to happen to you. Maybe you don't deserve it, huh? Maybe you're not good enough for that kind of fucking fabulous death."

Sean took out his cigarettes and passed them around. We all lit up. Then he said, "Do you know what Jeff sent me?"

"Yeah. I know."

"Do you know who killed him?"

"Yeah. I know that too."

"Tell me."

"Why the fuck should I?"

"Well, if you know, what are you gonna do about it?"

"Nothing. Everything. Cry out in the wilderness. Keep on fucking. What else is there, man? It's all sex. It's all about sex. The ones who have sex and the ones who don't and hate the ones who do. The ecstatics and the repressed. That's the war zone, man, except it's not our war, we don't want it, we don't give a shit, let them stay repressed, let them pray to God to stay repressed, who gives a fuck? But no. They want us all to die so we aren't here to remind them that we're fucking and they're not. They want to kill us for having orgasms and they're doing it and someday, man, there won't be an orgasm left on this planet. And then the world will end. Lights out."

"The celibates," I said.

"The frigid men and their frigid women. Blow us away, Christian soldiers. We're the devil incarnate. We're evil. We love each other. Kill us all."

"But one of them knew Jeff had those names."

"Too many people knew Jeff had those names. Because his asshole lover couldn't keep his mouth shut. He wanted the press. He wanted Queer Nation to out Slatley. But Jeff was too ethical, see. He gave Slatley the option to go public himself. Brendan would never give anybody an option. Brendan always wants what he wants, and he usually gets it. As you and I know, darling, from personal experience."

"But Slatley's name isn't even mentioned in the interview," Sean said, ignoring the last remark.

"I don't know about that," he said. "All I know is we had our little chat and next thing Miss Robert Rightwing is singing a new song."

He got up and started walking down the hill.

"Wait!" I said, "I'm Evan's sister, Evan from the hospice. I think you know him."

"Evan's sister? Shit. Well, look, I'm sorry I stole your stuff then. If I'd known you were his sister, I'd have been politer." He extended his hand. "Fuller's the name," he said.

"You called me at Evan's house. You left a message for Sean."

"Didn't know it was Evan's house. The number was on your checks."

"Well, you have our number then. If you ever decide you want to talk to us about Jeff . . ."

"What's Jeff to you, anyway?"

"He was Sean's friend," I said. "Isn't that enough?"

Fuller sat down again next to me. "OK," he said. "You want to deal with this shit, fine. Thursday night, close to midnight, I was leaving their place, Jeff and Brendan's. We'd had a meeting that night and we went to Bren's for a drink. I'm walking to 18th, I see Jeff coming down Collingwood. I see these two guys cross the street from the park and come up to him. It's dark, so I don't see what goes on between them, but then I see Jeff and these two men getting into a car. A black Buick. California plates. Next thing, he's a body dumped on Noe."

"You didn't tell the police about this?"

"No. I thought I'd wait for the cure." He got up again and started down the path, but he turned back. "See, Alexandra, it's real simple. I have maybe six months left on this planet. I don't have a minute for this bullshit. If it brought him back, sure. In a nano-second. But it doesn't bring anybody back. Nothing—no thing—brings anybody back. And I can promise you the wheels of justice are not going to start turning for these fuckers in my lifetime. Not that kind of justice anyway."

"So that was Fuller," I said. "What a guy."

"I'm glad you came, Alex," he said. "I'm glad you were here for this. So much for a random mugging, huh? So much for that shit."

"Those meetings between Jeff and Billy? You know, in the park? I bet it was Jeff who contacted Billy, not the other way around. He must have. He wouldn't have done this without talking to Billy about it first. Not if he was so ethical and . . ."

"He would have asked Billy. Of course. And Jeff could be very persuasive . . ."

"And Ted was dying, remember. So Billy was in pretty much the same place. Pissed off and helpless.

"So Billy gave him the big fish. Robert Slatley."

"Exactly. Then Jeff contacted Slatley and gave him the option of coming out himself. That way Billy was protected as a source. Jeff, too."

"Except too many people already knew about the interview, so they found Jeff and Billy and they killed them. That's what happened, Alex."

"But who? Because Slatley was outed already. The damage was done. And what about Lamont?"

"Lamont," he said. It was like a groan.

"Brendan called you by the way. From Michigan. About stuff you left in Jeff's car."

"I really didn't leave any stuff. I just wanted to find out where the car was. On Collingwood, right?"

"Right. But it got trashed."

"Of course. They had to search it."

"And they didn't find what they were looking for."

"No. So they went to Billy. And God knows what he told them before he died. Because Lamont was dead before he got cut up like that. But Billy wasn't. That's why I went back inside last night. To see."

I let that sink in for half a second and then I left it where it was in my head and jumped on. I didn't want to think about Billy Blake's murder. Or what he might have said while it was going on.

"How did Brendan sound?"

"He sounded OK."

"Maybe it hasn't hit him yet," Sean said. "Poor Brendan."

"Sean," I said, "we have to talk to the police now. We have to."

"Let's go," he said. "Let's get off this damn hill."

We walked down Caselli toward Castro Street. Caselli is a nice, quiet block. The houses on one side are built on a hill, so they have steep staircases. There's an alley that runs behind the houses, and staircases mid-block that let you cut by the houses and across the alley up to 19th. At the corner of Caselli and Douglass is another old hospital that's been turned into apartments.

"We have to stop in here for a minute," he said.

We went up the stairs to the front door and Sean opened a box. There was a phone inside. He dialed a number and said a few words into the receiver. The front door buzzed open.

"Now, be real cool, OK? Try not to say anything."

Inside, the building was like some kind of museum,

with dark woodwork, oriental rugs, old furniture and
fringed shades over the lamps, vases and knick-knacks
all over, as though it was someone's house. We went up
a set of stairs to the second floor and knocked on a door.
A young man opened it, but I didn't see him right off.
What I saw was the bed.

The bed filled the room. There was nothing else but
the bed. It was made of dark, heavy wood, mahogany
maybe, covered with black sheets, and on the bed, pretty
much bare-ass naked, Charlie with the nose ring, the
blond cappuccino drinker.

"Hey, Charlie," Sean said. "What's up?"

"My dick, as it happens. What's up with you, Sean?"

"Not that much."

"This is Steve," Charlie said, nodding to the doorman.
"Stevie, how about you go out and get us some beer,
huh?"

Steve, dismissed, left sullenly and slammed the door
behind him.

"Alex," Sean said, nodding to me.

Charlie nodded back. "Hold on," he said. He got up
stark naked and pulled on some shorts. Nice body. All
of it was very nice. "Now, Sean," he said, reclining back
languidly on the bed in his black boxers, "you wanted to
see me. Here I am. What's the big emergency?"

"No emergency. I just have something of Jeff's that I
heard you were interested in."

Charlie shook a cigarette out of his pack and lit it
with a classy silver Zippo. He squinted at us through the
smoke, looking like a cross between a sexy Calvin Klein
ad and a tom cat scrutinizing the pigeons.

"What sort of something?" he asked.

"Oh," Sean said, looking mildly annoyed. "Sorry, I
thought you knew all about it. Never mind then." He
started moving back toward the door.

"Wait!" Charlie said. "Do you know what it is?"

"Of course I do. More or less."

"What do you mean, more or less?"

"Well, I didn't *open* it. But I know what it is and what to do with it. Do you?"

"Yeah. I do. Look, let's cut the bullshit, Sean. You have something very important . . ."

"How do you know it's important?"

"Something very big, Sean. Mega. Now, what do you intend to do with it?"

"I intend to give it to the people I work for, the people Jeff worked for. The people Jeff intended it . . ."

"No, man. He didn't intend it for them. He wanted us to have it."

"Then why did he give it to me?"

"How do I know he gave it to you? Maybe you took it."

"Why would I take it?"

"To keep us from getting it . . . OK, look, you're here now. You changed your mind, right? You're going to give it us, aren't you? You're going to give it me." His voice was seductive and he was smiling at Sean, a very sweet, very warm smile. He was a man used to being irresistible.

"Actually, no. What I came over for is to ask you to talk to Brendan for me when he gets back. I know Jeff's supervisor will be asking him about it. I know he'll be concerned. He needs to know I have it and it's safe. I'm sure you'll see him sooner than I will. So I just wondered if you'd pass the word on to him. Tell him not to worry, that I'll be giving it to Lydia on Thursday. Would you do that for me?"

"Sure, Sean. If that's how you feel, you're sure you're doing the right thing . . ."

"I'm sure."

"Then that's cool," Charlie said.

"Thanks. I feel a lot better."

"No problem, man," Charlie said, waving us toward the door. "Take it easy, Sean. 'Bye, Alice."

"Later, Charlie," Sean said and waltzed me out the door.

I didn't say a word to him until we were on the street, walking toward my house.

"For a minute I thought you were going to give the interview to him."

Sean rolled his eyes at me. "Well, dear *Alice*, remember this: it's not over 'til the fat man farts. We have one more call to make."

"What are you up to? What are you *doing*?"

"Same sort of thing you were doing this afternoon, my lovely. Playing detective . . . You must really think I'm blind not to see you walking around behind me all day. God, Alexandra, please don't ever do that with a real killer, OK?"

"Well," I said, feeling only slightly humiliated and mortified, "at least you could tell me what's going on."

"Same as it ever was. I'm gonna find this fucker. I'm gonna find out who killed Jeff. That's what we're doing this week. Next week we can both look for jobs."

"If we survive this week, I think next week we should get married," I said, feeling on the brink of premenstrual madness, lunacy I think it's called.

"OK," he said. "Let's. I'll need a new car too. By the look of things."

We had passed my house and continued down the block to where Sean had left his car. It had been trashed too. Broken windows, broken doors, seats slit open. "Looks like they opened the trunk with a bazooka," he said. "Good thing Lydia always warned me not to leave interviews in the car."

*

"We can't go to your place," he said. "Where's Evan?"

"Hospice, I think. Why can't we go to my place?"

"Think about it. The cops found you from that letter. Well, the killers must have seen that same letter. And we don't know what Billy might have told them. So let's figure they know where you live. Call Evan. Then take your own car . . ."

"I don't have a car."

"Evan's then. Take Evan's car and go someplace safe. Please."

"Look, we're getting married next week, I'm staying very close to you."

"You're always very close to me. You don't have to be right next to me to be close to me."

"Yes I do," I said. "I'm not leaving."

"Jesus," he said. "Call Evan. I have a call to make too. Look, here are Siamese telephones." They were, too. Two public phone booths, joined at the back. "We'll be very close."

I couldn't talk to Evan. He was holding some dying man's hand and couldn't be disturbed. I left a message as clear and distinct as possible: Great danger at home. Tell Jake and both of you stay away tonight. Please. Alex.

"Where are we going now?"

"To see the third man."

"The third man? Explain."

"Three people—four counting myself—knew exactly how Lamont looked when he was dead. I mean, besides the cops, of course. Tom knew. I talked to him today, and he swore to me that he only told two other people. One was Charlie Coyote. The other was this third man, Harvey Siegel."

"But you forgot somebody. Lamont's killer knew."

"No, Alex. I didn't forget him. But whoever killed Lamont didn't kill Billy. You have to trust me on this, OK? It's not the same man. Therefore, the person who killed Billy has to be either one of these men or somebody *they* told. So we're going hunting."

"And the interview's the bait?"

"You got it. I tell everybody I have the interview and then we see who comes to get it."

"And then what do we do? Sean, *then what do we do?*"

"Well, we're not going to be there, silly. We're going to be sitting safe and sound at the windows in the front house with my very cool next-door neighbors, filming it. That's who I just checked in with. We set the cameras up this afternoon. Dress rehearsal. They're all ready for action. Or didn't I happen to mention to you that before I was an enumerator, I was a grad student. In video."

CHAPTER 20

Harvey Siegel, the third man, lived on Saturn Street, which is up among the other planetary streets: Mars, Uranus and Vulcan.

We couldn't use Sean's car, so we hiked it. Up 17th, which is itself a hefty climb. Then along Ord to the stairs at the foot of Saturn. More stairs. These stairs had gardens along them and at the top you got a terrific view of the city lights. But we weren't going to be sitting on a bench up here making out, not tonight. Besides, a homeless man had already taken possession of the bench.

Sean told me a few relevant things as we huffed and puffed up the hill. He had gone to see Joseph Angelicus to try to track Tom down. Joseph tended to know where everybody was at any given moment, and he had indeed known where Tom was staying. Evidently, Tom hadn't been without comfortable accommodations for long. He had been picked up by a rich older man (a stinking rich dirty old man, in Sean's words) and moved into his house on Corbett. That took him all of two days and two nights. The first night he had spent with Charlie; the second night, with Harvey Siegel.

Siegel was a therapist of some kind; Lamont had been one of his clients. Lamont had spoken about him to Tom, had trusted him, so when he dropped in on the Queer Nation meeting Thursday night and asked Tom if he needed a place to stay, Tom had gone home with him.

He was the sort of man who collected strays, and he had several young men living in his house. Tom hadn't liked them much, thought they were nerdy and weird, and after a night with Harvey had pretty much decided the same thing about him. Nonetheless, he had talked to him about Lamont. Harvey knew how to ask the right questions, and was the sort you opened up to. After all, that's how he made his living.

"One of those nurturing sorts of men," Sean said. "The New Age, Iron John, male bonding sort. Bonding, not bondage. I think Tom would have liked the bondage type better."

"Why would someone like that be interested in Billy's interview?"

"Maybe he wasn't. This is all just a hypothesis, Alex."

"Well, when we get there, what are we going to say?"

"I haven't figured that part out yet. Basically there's only one thing we need to do to test the theory. We just have to tell him we have it. That's all. We have it and this is where it is. That's it. Period. If he's not interested in the interview, he's off the hook."

"Oh," I said. "Like playing Clue."

"Exactly."

"And if he is interested, if he did know Billy, if he did kill Billy, then we're in deep shit, right there inside his house, aren't we?"

"No, m'am. Because we don't have it, do we? And whoever is killing people wants the interview."

"You'd think they'd figure we'd have given it to some-body by now."

"You'd think we would have."

"We haven't, I take it."

"It's very safe."

"Good. Don't tell me where it is in case they capture me and start pulling out my toenails."

"God, Alex, don't!"

Something in his voice scared me. What had he said about Billy? He wasn't like Lamont. Lamont had been dead when he got cut up. Billy hadn't been.

We had stopped in front of a big, rambling house with a Harley parked in the driveway.

"This is the place," Sean said. "And this is the routine. I go in and talk to him, you wait out here. If I don't come out in ten minutes or so, come and ring the bell. Just in case."

"In case what? . . . No, absolutely not. I'm going in with you."

"And what are we saying then? Alone, I could be looking for Tom, right? But with you . . ."

"Looking for Tom? How are you going to get the inter-view in there if you're looking for Tom?"

"I'm the enumerator for the AIDS study. I do the inter-views. I need to interview Tom, who I met at Lamont's and have been trying to track down ever since. I heard he was living here. If he's interested in Billy's interview, and he's as good at asking questions as I hear he is, he'll start quizzing me. See?"

I didn't want to wait outside, but I couldn't argue with his logic.

I waited outside.

Outside. The air was still mild. Over the lights of the city, hanging in the sky like a UFO, was a blimp, advertising some radio station. The sky itself was turning mauve, stars and planets were coming out, shining like diamonds, the crescent moon, lying on its back, was more golden than silver. A peaceful, perfect night.

I sat on the curb across the street from Harvey Siegel's house and prayed to all the gods and goddesses of earth and sky to protect my lover from evil.

I smoked a cigarette. I smoked another cigarette. I was going to finish this smoke and if Sean hadn't come out, I was going to ring Harvey's doorbell.

I was crushing out the butt when Sean came out the door and stood on the pavement looking up and down the street for me.

"A real curious man," Sean said as we descended the stairs at the end of the block.

"Curious as in odd or curious as in nosy?"

"Both. Attractive, old hippie look, you know, greying hair, pony-tail, that sort of thing. In his late forties. Very accommodating. Please sit down. Can I get you something? Tell me all about the study. Blah, blah. The phone rang three times while I was talking to him. Goes right into therapist mode. Maybe is always in therapist mode. Hot tub music playing. Very laid back and mellow. Very . . . I don't know, Reichean or something."

"What does that mean?"

"Oh, you know, like he wants to touch you and get you all orgasmic so you can release your libidinal energies and get centered and energized. But in a scientific and purely therapeutical way. Like he wouldn't get off on it himself, but he'd be helping you to realize your potential as a fully evolved being. I don't know. There's something cool and creepy about him, simultaneously."

"Did you meet his housemates, or whatever?"

"No. One of them was home, but he was in another room in some kind of trance or something and couldn't be disturbed. Both of them are eligible for the study. Of course, the household isn't, but that's beside the point. It gave me the opportunity to leave my name and home number. In case either of them wants to call."

"Did Harvey seem interested? I mean, overly interested?"

"Well, I don't know. He was curious. He asked the normal kinds of questions. He did ask me if I was the only one doing this. I lied and said yes. Then he got all concerned and nurturing and, Oh, it must be so difficult for you. How do you do it? Are you just in the Castro or all over the city? Very concerned and maternal. I hate that in a man."

"I don't mind it," I said. "Better maternal than paternal."

"Really?"

"Because paternal gets paternalistic real quick."

"Oh," he said. "Well, if I ever get paternalistic, you can beat me."

"I'll remember that," I said. "In fact, I'd like it in writing."

"Well, I'd like a coffee first. Café Flor, my love?"

"Café Hairdo? I don't know if we're coiffed for it."

"We're coiffed. We're tattooed and pierced and coiffed. They'll take our two bucks, don't worry."

By then we were sailing down 17th. It was all downhill from there.

Café Flor, or Café Hairdo as it is known by the snide, is on the corner of 16th and Market, an outdoor café in a little vine-covered enclosure, reminiscent of the tropics. I like sitting outside, I like the waiters, most of them, and the coffee's good. I like to sit and smoke and watch the life I'm not a part of happen all around me. I like going to the Flor and feeling alien and lonely, rejected, invisible and unloved. It's a real ego-trip.

It was amazing to walk into the Flor with Sean and suddenly be *visible*. Or maybe it was Sean who was visible and I just happened to be hanging on his arm. Several men stared at him and one said hi even though they didn't seem to know each other. They saw him, that's for sure. A form of acknowledgement, flirtation. Something I've been missing since Taos, that energy flowing at me from strangers. You get used to it and then when it's gone you feel oddly insubstantial, disembodied, sort of like a ghost.

I must have trembled or something because Sean squeezed my arm. "Are you OK?"

"Yeah," I said. "Scared to death but otherwise fine. What do we do next?"

"Order. Want something to eat?"

"Got any money?"

We counted up our change and decided we could order two coffees and one salad, leave a modest tip and have enough left for an emergency phone call. Perfect.

We were actually more than visible. We were sitting ducks.

Midway through our salad—one bowl, two forks,

please—I realized fully what he had done. He had put us in one of the most obvious spots in the neighborhood and there we were blissfully sharing some lettuce like nothing was happening.

He was so cool. He was talking about China again. He was entertaining me with stories. Making small talk. Asking me about Taos, about my career plans. Career plans! At a time like this?

"Well, if we're going to get married next week," he said, grinning at me.

"What? You want to know what my income potential is? Jesus."

I was basically a wreck.

"And then there's genetic testing. Any mental illness in your family?"

"My sister, yes. She married a moron."

"Morons by marriage don't count. Is he really?"

"He's a Republican," I said. "Isn't that the litmus test?"

"Not if you're upper class it's not. The upper class has to be Republican. It's the law."

"He's a Cold War aristocrat. Now he's scared Clinton will pull the plug and he'll have to sell one of his summer houses. I mean, it's tragic, isn't it?"

"Your sister married him, huh? Did she really fall in love with him?"

"I don't know," I said. It was impossible for me to think of Jeremy and falling in love simultaneously. The brain is a marvelous invention, but there are some things it just can't do. "You should come to the St. Francis with me on Friday and meet her. I'm her diversion between Jeff Koons and Lyman Jasper. Thrilling, isn't it?"

Sean laid his fork down and stared at me like I had just said something obscene. "Lyman Jasper?" he said.

"Yeah. Why?"

"Remind me. Who is Lyman Jasper?"

"He's the head of some right-wing group. Americans for Family Values or some . . ."

"Right. Wait. The bunch that bankrolled the Oregon referendum . . . or the one in Colorado. One of those anti-gay laws. That was Americans for Family Values. And they want to repeal California's gay rights law. And they're up in arms over gays in the military. That's them, that's Lyman Jasper. Oh my God, Alex. That's him!"

"Chill, Sean," I said. "I didn't marry the asshole. My sister did. And she's always been very straight. Very conser . . ."

"Alex, listen to me. Billy's interview. Page 9. 'They don't pay me for sex. They pay me to keep quiet about it. But do they think I'm going to keep quiet all my life? Do they think I'm that stupid? Well, Jasper does, that's for sure. He thinks he can keep paying my Visa bill and I won't say a word . . .'"

"Lyman and Jasper . . . I thought they were two different . . ."

"I can't believe this," he said.

I couldn't either. I almost wanted to laugh. I almost wanted to tell him he was out of his mind. Lyman Jasper, a closet case! Absurd.

Absurd and ridiculous. So ridiculous I flashed on the possibility that Billy Blake had been pulling Jeff's leg.

Then I remembered how Billy had died.

Then I felt that old terror again, that deadly fear.

"This can't be happening," I said.

I said it and then I glanced around. I had been dis-tracted. I had been in China, in Taos. I had been beguiled by love. I hadn't been watching who came into the café, or where they sat. I hadn't noticed who was sitting around us. I should be taken out and shot.

Charlie Coyote, now practically fully dressed, was just getting up from the table across the aisle right in front of me. He and Sean had been sitting practically back to back, close enough for him to have heard everything we'd said.

CHAPTER 21

"I think it's time to go to my place," Sean said. He was entirely too up, too into this. "Want to try Evan again?"

I said absolutely and left him at the table to use the phone inside. I called home first. No answer. That was good at least. I called the hospice and miracle of miracles, they put me on hold. A lifetime later, Evan came on the line.

"What the fuck?" Evan said, yelled, into my ear. "What's going on? I have two delirious messages from you. Are you on something, Alexandra?"

"Two? I only left one."

"Which one? The don't go home tonight one or the I forgot my keys, leave the door unlocked one?"

"Someone called you and told you to leave the door unlocked? That wasn't me, Evan. You didn't do it, did you?"

"How could I? I'm here."

"Can you stay there? Can you sleep there tonight?"

"Don't be ridiculous! This is a hospice not a bed and breakfast. Do you think you could tell me what's going on exactly?"

I tried. I told him how Sean believed the same people who killed Jeff also killed Billy, how he was trying to flush out the killers, using the interview as bait, how he had talked to Harvey Siegel and Charlie, how he had his ad hoc film crew waiting back on Parnassus.

"OK, Zand. Now listen to me." This was Evan at his most adamant. "The cops have been all over the Castro all day today, and they've been hitting the bars tonight. They're asking questions about Lamont's boyfriends . . ."

"I thought they'd done that already."

"Well, this time they have a description of one of them they're particularly interested in finding. Late twenties, dark hair, pierced eyebrow, geometric tattoo on his left arm . . . Sound familiar, Zand? Now, I want you to come here right away, by yourself. I can't say this more *forcefully*. You have to be with me now. Lose him. He's bad news."

"Did you talk to them? I just need to know, Evan."

"No. I just got the word from the street. But somebody will, eventually, because everybody wants to get Lamont's killer. And Billy's. Everybody . . . Be here in half an hour, Zand, or I'll call Kagehiro myself. I swear I will."

I knew enough not to argue. I said, "I'm in North Beach at the moment. It'll take me more than thirty minutes to . . ."

"One hour. One hour, Zand. I'll wait here for you. OK?"

"OK," I said.

I smiled at the man who had been waiting patiently to use the phone. It was an entirely false smile. I just didn't know what to do next, but I figured Sean would have a plan. He was resourceful. He'd figure it out.

I walked outside, back to our table.

Three gay men were sitting at it laughing and drinking coffee. Sean was gone.

I stood staring at them until one of them paid attention to me, the madwoman of the Café Flor.

"Can we help you?" he asked, like he was the Princess of Wales. I wanted to punch him in the face.

"There was a man sitting here ... Did you see him go?"

They exchanged little smiles, like, Oh, Mary! Her date walked out on her. Boo-hoo. Now I really wanted to hit them with something.

"A real cutie, nice gold ring up here?" one of them said, pointing to his eyebrow. "He left. He's gone."

"By himself, or did he run into his friends?"

"Oh, I think he saw some cute bottom walking by and . . ."

I reached around the table and picked up my big black bag with the camera in it and my book and all my very heavy shit. "Thanks," I said, and then I accidentally swung it up just a little too hard and it just got out of control, and, Oh, so very sorry, I said, as it smashed Mr. Cute Bottom right in the face. So terribly sorry.

Dickhead.

He had to be going back to his place. He must have figured I'd know that's where he went. Or maybe he saw someone . . . Or maybe he saw the cops.

It just wasn't like him to ditch me like that.

Or was it?

I was marching past tables toward the exit to the street when I nearly collided with a waiter whose purple lipstick and eyeliner matched the color of his hair and who had more rings on his face than I had in my ears.

"Oh, hon-ey!" he said as I brushed by him. "You're the one with Sean?"

I stopped in my tracks.

"He said to meet him on the corner."

"What corner?" I said.

The waiter shrugged. "This one, I guess," he said, and waltzed away.

The Flor is on a corner, it's true. But there are many

corners right here on Market and 16th ... and so far as I could see Sean wasn't standing on any of them.

But cars were going by on Market and it was too dark to see who was standing on the other side of the street. I waited where I was for two lights. No sign of Sean crossing Market or on any corner within my range of sight. Where was he? I was not really present for a few seconds, wondering where he could be, where to go next, and that's when the Mercedes pulled up in front of me and the man jumped out and opened the rear door.

"Get in!" Sean said. "Hurry! We're holding up traffic."

"Nice car," I said, leaning over the front seat to check out the driver. He was real young and a total grunge. This was obviously not his car.

"Borrowed," Sean said. "Alex, this is Tom."

We sort of nodded to each other.

"Where am I dropping you?" Tom asked.

"Why don't we drop you and keep the car for awhile? He's out of town, right?"

"Yeah. OK. Drop me anywhere on Haight."

"It'd be safer to stay inside."

"Hey, man. It'd be safer to be dead ... I been thinkin' about what you asked me before. How much detail, you know, I ever went into with anyone? I didn't think I said too much, but then I remembered the camera. See, I took photos of him. I remember I did, but I wasn't sure how the camera worked. He'd been taking pictures in the apartment so I just took more, you know, I didn't fuck with any of the numbers or anything. Just left it like it was and took the pictures. Then I put it in my bag and I brought it with me to your place, right? Then I brought it to Charlie's and then to the meeting and then to Harve's. But somewhere I lost the camera. One of those places, 'cause I don't have it now."

We were at the corner of Divis and Haight. "Which way are you heading?" Sean asked.

"Down," he said and turned right.

This was the part of the street where we had met Shira the Shaman and first heard the name Fuller and it seemed like years ago, not just two days.

"Fun to be cruising for a change and not be cruised," Tom said. "So this is how we all look from inside a Mercedes, huh?"

How it looked was bizarre, surreal, like a scene from a Fellini movie, *Satyricon* maybe. The street so dark, people standing around, hookers, dealers, lost boys, run-aways, selling or buying, getting ready to sleep on the sidewalks. Over the storefronts, the grey wooden apart-ments with their bay windows, lights on, people living every kind of life, every income bracket probably, you could tell from the gates on the street and from the look of the windows ... flop house or condo, cheek by jowl. But, Jesus, so many kids on the street. And, yeah, you could cruise down in your black Mercedes and pull up at the curb and roll your window down, say a few words, have your choice of bodies for the night, or the hour, or for as long as it took. You could see them watching the car, see their curiosity, their interest. Hunger and hate. Or maybe not hate. Maybe that was coming from me.

"I'll get out here," he said. "I got a friend in that palace," he nodded toward one of the slummier buildings on the block. "I'll hang with him."

"Later, man," Sean said, as the driver got out and Sean slid over to take his place. "Thanks for the car. What do you want me to do with it? Bring it back there?"

The kid was already distracted by a group gathering on the corner. "Uh ... no. Keep it at your place. I'll call you. He's not back 'til Sunday. No rush ... Hey, before you go, you wanna get high?"

Sean shook his head and pulled away.

"Hey, wanna go for a ride?" he asked me. "Wanna climb in front? Wanna get high?"

"That was Lamont's boyfriend?" I asked, climbing over the seat.

"Yeah. Seriously, let's tool around a little. Let's go someplace." He made a u-ey and headed back up Haight.

"Sure," I said.

"There's a joint in the ashtray, if you want some. A mild-mannered drug, but it does the job for the granola brains of the world, myself for example. Could you light it up for me?"

I lit the joint, took a drag and passed it to him. We kept passing it from stop light to stop light all the way up Haight. I had no idea where we were going until he turned on Clayton and then onto Twin Peaks Boulevard. Climbing up to the top of the world, or our little corner of it anyway.

"Evan said the cops were looking for you," I said, in between tokes.

"For me?"

"Someone who fits your description, anyway. That's what he said. He also said if I wasn't at the hospice in an hour he was going to talk to them."

"Hmm," he said. "What do you mean, talk?"

"Give them your name, I guess."

"He really wonders about me, doesn't he?"

"What about your friend? What photos was he talking about?"

"He took photos of Lamont, I think. And then he left the camera at either Charlie's or Harvey's."

"Or your house."

"It's not at my house."

"What did you mean that the person who killed

Lamont didn't kill Billy. I mean, how exactly do you know that unless you know who exactly killed Lamont."

"I do know who exactly killed Lamont. But I can't tell you, Alex. But I know this much: it was an accident and he didn't kill anybody else."

"An accident! How can you slit somebody open and call it . . ."

"That's not how it happened," he said. "It was an accident. There was a fight. Domestic violence. Lamont got hit with a paperweight and it cracked his skull. That's how Lamont died. The rest was . . . art."

"*Art?*"

"It's hard to explain, I know."

"Why are the cops looking for you then?"

"I told you, I was there. Someone saw me, I guess."

"How much of it were you there for?"

"Not much," he said. "Look, if you have any doubts at all, I can just take you . . . wherever you want to go. To the hospice, if that's what you want."

I was pretty stoned, and it can make you paranoid. It can make you think people are evil just as easily as it can make you love them. But I wasn't paranoid of Sean. I believed him.

"Take me to the top of the world," I said. "That's where I want to go."

That's where we went.

Up on top of the world, there are always cars parked. Always. The parking lots up on Twin Peaks are never empty, no matter what time of night you go up, what time of year. This night there weren't many cars, but we wanted absolute privacy, I guess, because we drove around for awhile searching for the perfect spot. We looked out at the city from all the directions and then settled into a parking spot looking east down the wide, bright swath of Market Street toward downtown and the Bay Bridge and the lights of the East Bay twinkling over at us. The buildings downtown were still festooned for the holidays, the bigger ones outlined in lights like a storybook city. Lights spanning the Bay Bridge made it look like a great ornament, a necklace of diamonds laid out across the dark water. It was so beautiful, a city of lights, and the crescent moon hanging like a bauble over it all, like a blessing.

"Want to get out?" he asked.

"No," I said. "I want to kiss you."

We kissed for a long time.

"This is a gay car," he whispered to me. "I don't know if it can handle the kind of deviance you have in mind."

"Breeders have rights too," I whispered back.

"Did the breeders bring condoms with them?"

"Doesn't the car come with a dispenser?"

"Probably, but I don't know which button to push."

I put my hand on his beautiful hard cock and said, "I think we can handle this situation without latex."

"Look in the glove compartment," he said.

They were there, along with lubricant and poppers. The full panoply.

So it happened that ten minutes later I was straddling him, facing the rear window, and very close to coming, when I saw another car drive past us and then back up. It cut its lights, and turned in right behind us, blocking us. Two men got out of the car, one from each side, and started toward us.

I pulled away from Sean and pushed him over to the driver's side, yelling something to him, like "Behind us!" or "Drive!" but he'd seen what was coming down too, through the rear-view mirror and he started the engine up in a second. He put it in reverse and smashed hard into the car behind us. The Mercedes was a tank and did some serious damage to the front end of the other car. He didn't hesitate, he turned the wheel to the left and shot us forward, over the curb, almost to the edge of the precipice. For a heartbeat I thought we weren't going to make it, we were going to roll over right down the side of the mountain, but he made the turn, we hit pavement, and burned rubber through the parking lot and onto Twin Peaks Boulevard. The road up there is narrow and curved, one long curving descent from the top of Twin Peaks to Clayton far below. We were fast, but the other car, smashed front end and all, was coming along behind us.

"Hold on!" he said, like I wasn't. "We're going down the other way. Shit!"

I couldn't see where we were, but I figured he meant we were heading toward Portola. Easy to get turned around up there, but we were still ahead of them. We hit Portola and Sean turned left and then left again. Now we were on a series of blocks that curved around the south slope of Twin Peaks, streets with original names like Sun View and Dawn View and Glen View and Long View lined with those new condo-apartments that looked like they wouldn't hold up in a stiff wind, that were already cracking and falling apart but that people paid enormous rents for so they could sit up near the top of the world and look down at the lights. A maze of streets, but we kept turning left, hoping to lose them and not get lost ourselves.

"I think we're OK," he said slowing down. "Where the fuck are we?"

Crestline Drive. New apartments to the right, undeveloped open space to the left. We came around a bend and the road ended. Just stopped. A fence, a long drop, the lights below.

"Shit," he said. We made a u-ey, cut the lights, pulled

on our clothes. "Well, we'll see their lights before they see us," he said. "Are you OK?"

He'd no sooner said it than we saw headlights. "Hold on!" he said. He kept his lights off and floored it. They had their brights on; Sean hit his brights just as we got close. We side swiped them a little, but got by, took the next curve at an amazing speed but there was a second car waiting there for us, blocking the street. We had to hit it, we couldn't stop. We were going to die in a car crash. Shit!

Sean steered the Mercedes to the right, away from the curve, away from the street. I couldn't believe he was doing this, but he steered right over the curb onto the grass. The Mercedes fishtailed, but only a little, she really clung tight to the road, or grass in this case, it almost looked like she was going to take us right around and back onto the street, but the grass was high and the terrain steep. We'd lost speed and we were hitting rocks. Sean turned the wheel to the left, to try to get us back on solid ground before we bogged down, but a boulder got in our way. He braked and put the car in reverse, but the poor Mercedes wasn't a four-wheel drive and she was good and stuck in grass and rock. We didn't have time to tease her out. We'd have to run for it.

"I'll go down, you go up," he said. I didn't argue. I set off running up to the top of the rise. Very quickly I realized nobody was on my heels so I stopped and turned around. I couldn't see anything much. The Mercedes, yes, with her motor running and her brights still on; the other cars in the road. It occurred to me they could be cops, but then there were no blue lights, no sirens, no voice over the loudspeaker ordering you to pull over. I strained my eyes for movement and then I saw it, two figures in black running, the second car swinging around, peeling out down the street, two more black-clad men getting out, joining the chase.

I was paralyzed. I stood there like an agoraphobic, heart racing, not knowing what to do. Then I took a deep breath and ran too.

CHAPTER 22

I ran back down the hill toward Sean. One of the men had tackled him and the other two were running toward him. It was horrible, watching it happen, knowing there was nothing I could do.

I could make a run for the Mercedes.

But I didn't. I crouched down behind a rock. It was so quiet up here, no traffic, no people. It was so quiet except for the wind in the grass that I could hear everything. I could hear them panting. I could hear the snap of latex gloves being put on. I could hear the sound of tape being pulled off the roll. And the one holding Sean down swearing, I could hear that too.

"Tape him up and throw him in the car," one of them said. "We're taking him to his place."

"Jesus Christ. Let's do it here."

"Dunbar says do it there. So we do it there. Anyway he has it. We have to get it from him first."

"Fuck," the one on the ground said. "OK, faggot, we're going for a ride."

Two of them pulled him up. I couldn't make out their faces, but I could see they were wearing black and had smooth, pale hands, hands encased in latex gloves.

"What about the girl?" one of them said.

"Let the cunt go. For now."

They dragged Sean to the light-colored car that was idling in the street and pushed him in. One got in the back seat with him, the other two got in the front. The car drove off, and the car behind it, the one that had pinned us in up on Twin Peaks, followed.

I got to see it real well as it passed under the street light. It was a black Buick with California plates.

As soon as the cars were gone I ran back to the Mercedes. I started it and tried backing up very slowly. A miracle: slow worked. I backed away from the boulder and got it back onto the street.

They were taking him to his place.

I had to get there before they did.

Market to Clayton to Parnassus. A straight run. They were at most five minutes ahead of me. They couldn't afford to get picked up for speeding; I, on the other hand, would be so glad to see a San Francisco cop I'd hug the man—or woman. So I had nothing to lose. I drove like all hell was chasing me, down Market, right through two red lights, onto Clayton, running stop signs, almost running over pedestrians, I didn't care.

I got to Parnassus and Clayton just as they did. I saw them cruise down Parnassus looking for Sean's building. They'd probably double park out front and carry him in. I went half a street over to the alley that ran behind Sean's house and drove down it, parking the Mercedes a few doors away from his.

I opened the glove compartment and fished around among the condoms, lubricant and poppers. I hadn't imagined it. I had really seen it up on Twin Peaks. It was really there, way in the back. Every Mercedes owner has to have one, especially in San Francisco in this age of car-jackings: in this case, a nice little Smith and Wesson automatic.

Loaded.

I got out of the car and crept along the side of Sean's house. I had a perfect view of the walkway from the street. The light in the garden was on tonight, and I wondered if his front neighbors were still awake, waiting for him to come in and man his video camera out their side windows. But I couldn't count on them. I couldn't count on anything but my aim, not exactly a safe bet but all I had.

New Mexico is such a great macho place, the old West, cowboys and Indians, pick-ups with rifles in the back. My Indian boyfriend was a shooter, like the rest of them, and he couldn't live with a woman who had never held a gun in her life, much less shot one. We remedied the situation with frequent afternoons at the target range. I could shoot any sort of gun now, not that I had ever wanted to. But shooting a gun is not the same as hitting a target with it.

I had just taken up position at the corner of Sean's house when they appeared at the street end of the walkway. One man in front, two coming behind, holding Sean up like he was drunk or something. The other guys were probably parking the cars.

I had never shot at anybody before. I watched my hand shake as I held the gun and I wondered if I could really do it and what if by accident I killed one of them, what if by accident I hit Sean instead. What if I didn't hit anything and they rushed me and killed me too.

As they passed under the walkway light, I saw that Sean had tape over his eyes and mouth. I had one instant flash of Billy Blake's body hanging in his doorway and took a breath, aimed and pressed the trigger. And kept pressing it.

Three men down.

Thank God, the right three.

Sean was standing, hands tied behind him, blind and mute.

I ran up to him and pulled the tape off his face.

The three men down were writhing in pain, crying and swearing. It hurts, I guess, to get shot in the balls. Though I swear I was really aiming for their knees.

I kissed him and untied his hands.

"Where are the other ones?"

"In the cars. God, I love you," he said.

"Of course you do," I said. "I just saved your life."

He asked me for the gun and I gave it to him. He squatted down next to one of the men and held the gun right at his face.

"Dunbar. Who is he?"

"I don't know. God, help me! I'm shot!"

"Look, I'll call an ambulance as soon as you tell me about Dunbar."

"He pays us."

"First name? What's his first name?"

"Randy. Randy Dunbar."

"He paid you to kill Billy Blake? Come on, or we'll leave you here. You'll bleed out in this alley, man. Did Dunbar pay you to . . ."

"Yeah. OK? Yeah, he did."

"And Jeff Taylor?"

"Yeah."

"For the interview?"

"Yeah . . . Come on. Jesus Christ, please. I need a doctor."

"And who does Dunbar work for? Who's behind this?"

"Don't know. I don't fucking know."

"You don't want that doctor real bad, do you?"

"I know," one of the other men said. "I'll tell you. Man, I'm gonna die. You call emergency right away, OK? You call right now, I'll tell you . . . Dunbar is a lieutenant in the army . . ."

We heard the sound together, car doors slamming right in front. It could be the cops, but I wasn't taking the chance and neither was Sean, who had already jumped and grabbed my hand. We ran down the passage to the alley and the Mercedes parked there. At the end of the passage, I turned my head and looked back. Two men in black holding guns in their hands were running from the street toward the three I had shot.

They weren't cops.

We got in the Mercedes and drove. Sean was at the wheel. We didn't talk, I didn't ask him where we were going. I closed my eyes and tried to find my soul, cowering somewhere in my body. How could I have shot those men? What if they died? Though they'd killed Jeff and Billy, so it wasn't like I'd killed innocent people, if I killed them at all. I never hit the target on center at the shooting range. But then I'd been a lot closer tonight than I ever was to a paper target or a can on a log.

When the car stopped, I opened my eyes. He had brought me to the hospice, to Evan.

We sat out front for a while first, just holding each other.

"Are you OK?" I asked him, feeling him all over, just to be sure. "Did they hurt you?"

"A bruise or two. Nothing much. I'm fine. Really."

"Oh, God," I said. "They were going to kill you."

"Yeah. Weird, huh? But we know more now . . ."

"Sean! They were going to *kill* you!"

"They called this guy Dunbar from a cellular phone in the car. To tell him everything was cool . . . They thought I'd give them the interview and then they'd kill me and that would be that. Fuckers."

"The army," I said. "The *army*."

"That is what he said, isn't it? I did hear right?"

"You did. They didn't seem very professional for the army. You'd think the army would be able to catch you, if they wanted you bad enough."

"Well, those losers aren't the army. They're just hired hands. But nobody named Randy Dunbar was mentioned in Billy's interview. So who are they really protecting?"

"We could look through it again. Get all the names and see which of them are in the army. I bet there's a listing or something . . ."

"You were magnificent back there, by the way."

"Oh," I said. "Thanks."

"Alex, I mean it. You were totally incredible. You were amazing."

He kissed me. I kissed him. I'd never been so in love in my life. I would have thrown myself in front of a truck for him. Or, given the situation at hand, a tank.

"We should have gotten their names at least."

"Oh," I said. "We did OK. For amateurs."

"I'm getting a little worried about this car. I don't want Tom getting in any trouble. And I'm not going to be home tomorrow, obviously. So how about we ask if we can borrow Evan's and bring this baby home. She deserves a rest."

"And the gun, too. I don't know what to do with the gun."

"Put it back. You think those guys are going to the cops with this? I sure don't."

I reloaded from the Mercedes's bullet stash, wiped the gun off with my shirt and very carefully, with my hands wrapped in a scarf, replaced it in its little nook in the glove compartment. We checked for other tell-tale signs of our joyride. No bottles or trash in the backseat. Only a used condom which Sean remembered he had tossed somewhere during our high-speed chase and went searching for on the floor. It was too dark to check out the back end, so I was willing to say it was all OK and leave it at that.

I was too tired to think.

We strolled into the hospice thinking about a cup of hot tea and a nice hug from Evan, not necessarily in that order.

And walked right into the waiting arms of Homicide Detective Kagehiro who arrested Sean on the spot for the murder of Lamont Bliss.

CHAPTER 23

"How could you do that?" I wailed at Evan. "How could you call the cops on Sean? How *could* you?"

"If he's innocent, like you say he is . . ."

"Oh, right. Oh, right, sure. If he's innocent, he'll get off. Oh, sure, Evan. What fucking country are you living in?"

"They have evidence, Zand."

"Right. Well, I just shot three men tonight . . . Why don't you call the cops on me, too?"

And then I couldn't take it anymore and I sat down on one of the antique wing-back chairs in the beautiful blue and white Victorian parlor of the hospice where lovers and friends and relatives cried night after night and I cried too, like I had just lost my brother or my best friend.

Or both.

They made me tea, Evan and one of the other hospice workers named Chris who was good at listening and hand-holding, and had just had a good cry himself and so was extremely sympathetic. They clucked around me like mother hens and I wept and made a huge mess with tissues and tea bags and told them everything.

"What do you want us to do?" Chris asked when I was finished sobbing and carrying on. "Or rather, what do we do first?"

"Get Sean out of jail," I said. "Call Elizabeth."

"Elizabeth? Do you think Jeremy is going to put up bail money for . . ."

"My fiancé, yes."

"Your *what*?"

"You heard me. And Elizabeth has her own money, doesn't she? How much can it be?"

"For a first degree homicide? A lot. If they even set bail. They may not."

"I'll call her. Can you at least find out . . ."

"I'll find out," Chris said. "My lover's a lawyer. He can find out what's happening. I'll call him right now."

I wanted to kiss him.

"I don't see how they can even hold him," I said to Evan while Chris made his call. "Don't they need evidence anymore?"

"They have it. I talked to Kagehiro, Zand. They had a warrant."

"What? What do they have?"

"They have his fingerprints in Lamont's apartment. They have a witness who saw him going in the night Lamont was killed, and the next night, too. And they have an affidavit from another witness who swears that a few days after the murder Sean had in his possession a camera that belonged to Lamont."

"Who's the witness?"

"They're certainly not going to tell us who the witness is."

"And where's this camera now?"

"Kagehiro has it. Sean left it with this witness, and the witness turned it in to the cops. So see how bad it looks? They have him in the apartment, they have his fingerprints, they have this camera of Lamont's that somebody says he had, and he also knew Billy and he also knew Jeff . . ."

"*Evan*! Weren't you listening to me? Those men that were after us tonight. They kidnapped Sean. They admitted that they killed Billy and Jeff. We have to find this Randy Dunbar . . ."

"OK. OK. But think like a cop for a minute. They're going to charge Sean with Lamont's murder and they'll assume the other two are related . . . Look, there can't be two or three killers hitting gay men in one neighborhood in one week. There's got to be only one. That's how the cops are going to look at this, and that's how they're going to deal with it. They'll link him to all three. And they can, Zand. That's my point. He was the last person to see Jeff alive, and he was at Billy's the night he was killed."

"So was I."

"That's right. And he fucking better keep you out of it."

"You think he's a killer, but you want him to be honorable about it. Good, Evan."

"I didn't say I thought he was a killer. I don't think he's a killer. I called the cops because I was worried about you. And I was right to worry. So now he's in police custody, nobody's going to try to kill him, are they? He's out of the loop, Zand. He's as safe as he can be. So, let's let him stay safe for awhile and you and I take up the fucking torch and find Randy Dunbar, OK?"

"Oh, Evan," I said, hugging him. "Thank you."

"Well, somebody's got to keep an eye on you while

you go playing Joan of Arc... Are you serious about marrying this guy?"

"As far as Elizabeth is concerned, I am. I don't know. Maybe."

Too much was happening all at once. I couldn't think beyond finding Randy Dunbar. It was a name at least. For the first time, an actual person. A name.

"So we find this Dunbar person," Evan said, reading my mind. "In the army."

"And the guy who had the camera. Because he's lying, so he has to be involved in this somehow. I bet it's either Charlie Coyote or Harvey Siegel."

"Harvey Siegel. Now there's a character. Well, first things first. How about some sleep. Then we'll call Elizabeth. Chris said I could stay at his place tonight. I assume that includes you."

"Absolutely," Chris said, coming into the parlor. "And Paul says he'll go down to the lock-up in the morning and talk to Sean. They're still processing him. No word about a bail hearing yet, but we'll know in the morning."

So Sean had a lawyer and all I had to do was get some bucks from my sister.

And find Randy Dunbar.

"You could just talk to Kagehiro," Evan said as we were settling in on the futon convertible bed in Chris and Paul's living room. "Just tell him everything. Wouldn't that work?"

"If Sean decides to tell him, that's fine," I said. "But I'm not going to volunteer anything. Not until I talk to Sean."

"And I suppose there's a good reason..."

"I don't know," I said. "I can't think." And I rolled over and went instantly to sleep.

We got up in what seemed to be five minutes but was actually several hours. Evan had to go home and get some things for work. He had to at least put in an appearance after taking the day off, and we both wanted to see if anything had happened to our house during the night.

We met Paul briefly over coffee. He was older than I expected, with short white hair but not a line on his face, cosmetic surgery or else there was a portrait of him somewhere aging like crazy. I gave him some messages for Sean, like that I'd come and see him as soon as they let me and that we'd get the money together to get him out. And that Evan was on our side. And that we were looking for Dunbar. And what should I do with the Mercedes.

"And tell him I adore him," I said. "If you get a chance."

Paul grinned at me and for one second he stopped looking like a lawyer and transformed into a normal gay man. I felt much better.

We drove the Mercedes from Paul and Chris's to our house with a certain trepidation—or at least I did. I expected the house to be trashed, threatening words written in blood scrawled on our walls, that sort of thing. But no. It was as though nothing had happened during the night at all.

Of course I had injured three of them. Maybe they were in retreat.

Evan changed his clothes and collected his briefcase. I made more coffee and put on a Marianne Faithfull album, *Working Class Hero*, to get geared up for calling my sister in Marin.

"What are you doing today?" Evan asked me. "Where will you be at 1? I can get off at 1 and meet you."

"I'm going to wait here until Paul calls and then call Elizabeth and then return the car and then . . . I guess I call the army and find out how I can locate my long-lost uncle, Randy Dunbar. Just to see what they say."

"I don't want you to stay here," he said. "Return the car and then take my car to Marin. Please? I'll check out the army. We have researchers at work with time on their hands, and there's always the library. Or I'll call one of the bases. I'll find out where Randy Dunbar is. In fact, if you still have that list of names from the interview, I'll see if I can scare up any other army suspects. Then I'll call you at Elizabeth's and you can drive in and pick me up."

The thought was appalling but I agreed. I had to give Evan something. A little peace of mind for the morning wouldn't hurt. Even if it wasn't going to be reality-based. But then, what peace of mind is?

I was waiting for the lawyer to call when someone knocked on the front door. I checked through the window.

Tom.

"Oh," I said, opening the door. "Your car!"

"Not my car. Can I . . ."

I opened the door wider and let him come in.

He was very skinny, sallow, underfed or ill. He was wearing a Metallica t-shirt, a flannel shirt wrapped around his waist, torn jeans and engineer boots. He couldn't have been more than sixteen, and that might be stretching it.

"I heard about Sean," he said. "You have to understand. I can't go to the cops."

"I understand," I said. "Sean understands too. He's not ratting on you."

"He won't, will he?"

"I don't think so, no."

"But if they convict him? What then?"

He was shaking. Just shaking like he was having a fit or something. I said, "Are you cold? Do you want some coffee?"

"No. Yeah. Yeah, if you have some."

I did and poured him a mug.

"See, it's like this. I'm gonna die soon anyway. In a few months maybe, when it gets bad, when it's all over with me, then I'll confess. Tell him, OK? Tell him. I swear I'll do it then. I swear."

I sat very still at the table and watched him shake and try to get the coffee mug to his mouth without spilling it. I knew exactly how Sean had felt with this kid. I understood exactly. You wanted to take care of him. You wanted to deny what he was saying and make him a good meal or take him clothes shopping or to the movies. He did that to you. But he was saying . . . what was he saying?

"See, Alex. I gotta live every day of my life. I gotta live now, I can't let them bury me yet . . . Sean understands. I said, Man, I can't give you nothin' for this. There's nothin' I have. Undying friendship, twenty-six weeks' worth, maybe? You want it? Oh, yeah, and you can come to my funeral . . ." He put his fists up to his eyes. Tears were streaming down his face, but he put his fists up to his eyes like he wanted to push all the tears back. "I didn't mean to kill him," he sobbed. "Oh Jesus, I miss him so much."

CHAPTER 24

I let him sob for awhile at the table. I brought him tissues and cigarettes and more coffee. I didn't say anything. I just let him shake and sob and cry.

Of course Sean had given him money and all the grass in his house. Of course he had promised not to tell anyone what he had done to Lamont. He might even be willing to take the rap for this murder rather than turn this kid in.

Sean had a very strong, very evolved soul.

Not me.

"Listen, Tom," I said. "We have to find out who had Lamont's camera. The cops have it now. But who gave it to them? Because whoever did is saying that Sean had it, and he didn't, did he?"

"Whoever has the camera has my bag, too, with all my shit in it."

"What kind of bag?"

"A blue Polo. Lamont gave it to me. He had two of them, so he just gave me one. Lamont was cool like that. Gave you things. Just like that."

"What did you have in it?"

"Spray paint, markers, drugs. My meds, which I stopped taking anyway. A Swiss Army knife. A book or two. Oh, and my ring. Lamont gave me a ring. I don't wear rings. I wore it on a chain for while. Then I just stuck it in my bag . . . Things get lost too easy. You can't get attached to things. Fuck things. But people . . . You get attached to people and then they get lost too . . ."

He cried some more.

He was a mess.

He was as bad as I was.

Slowly, painfully, we reconstructed Tom's life over the days between the time he had accidentally hit Lamont too hard and cracked his skull and the time he noticed he didn't have his Polo bag.

He had done some extraordinary things during those three days.

He had spent hours turning Lamont—his body anyway—into a floral design, a shrine to Lamont's love and his own love for Lamont. He had strung Lamont's body up on the bedposts and brought plants and twisted them around the bedposts so the whole bed looked like an arbor. He had taken flowers and positioned them around the bed. He had taken photographs, used up the roll. But then, when it still didn't look right, when Lamont was still Lamont and not the essence of plant life itself, he had taken the florist knife and made a very narrow slit in Lamont's abdomen and put flowers inside him.

Once he did that, he couldn't stop doing it, until Lamont's whole body was bursting with flowers.

Until the insides of Lamont's body began bursting out too.

On the second night, he had gone out for awhile. He had been looking for thread, for heavy nylon thread, to sew Lamont up again. Surgical thread. He had met some friends and shot up. He had gotten pretty high. He went back to Lamont's building and up the stairs and inside . . . he didn't really know how long he'd been gone. He walked into the bedroom and saw his dead lover suspended from the bedposts surrounded by flowers with his insides hanging out and he forgot who had done it. He forgot and he freaked.

And sick and hysterical he came out from vomiting in the bathroom and there was Sean, staring up at Lamont as though, in Tom's words, he was seeing God.

Sean had taken him home.

From Sean's house he had gone to Charlie's and from
Charlie's to a Queer Nation meeting and from the Queer
Nation meeting to Harvey's . . .

"And I still had my bag!" he yelled, jumping up. "Yes!
I still had it then. During the night I snuck out and tagged
the side of Harvey's house. You'll see it there, on the
side. Bliss, that's my tag. So I tagged the damn house
and then I split and I left the fucking bag there . . . I left
it at Harvey's!"

Tom took his new Sugar Daddy's Mercedes and went
home.

Immediately after that, Paul called and told me Sean
was OK and loved me too. And had himself a lawyer.
And not to worry about money. Bail hadn't been set yet.
If they set bail at all, which they might not, it was going
to be hefty. Steep. Astronomical. You only needed 10 per
cent, but 10 per cent of a million is still a fucking lot of
bread.

I was so tempted to tell him what Tom had told me,
but I didn't. I just told him he was a saint and adorable
on top of it and I'd get the money somehow.

"Sean's expressed real concern about your safety,
Alex," Paul said. "He indicated to me that you might be
in serious danger, especially if you stay in your house. It
would make him feel a million per cent better if he knew
you were safe. Is there someplace you can go?"

I told him my sister lived in Mill Valley and I'd be
going there. I even gave him Elizabeth's phone number
so he could call me, to make it official.

It was a conspiracy to get me to Marin.

And then I did the most awful, hideous, painful, morti-
fying thing a woman can do: I called my rich older sister
because I'm not too proud to beg.

She wasn't home.

Harvey Siegel wasn't home either, which I found sur-
prising since his office was right in his house. I went all
around the house ringing doorbells, the front doorbell,
the side doorbell, the bell on the office doorway in the
back. On my exploration around the building I passed a
newly painted spot where I could still detect a shadow
of spray-painted letters, the ghost-image of Tom's tag:
BLISS.

I was just starting to ring bells again—indulging in
that Aries tendency to ram your head against brick
walls—when a pale, pasty, disheveled young man
appeared at the door and squinted out at me.

Len the Celibate.

"What?" he said.

"I have an appointment with Harvey," I lied. "It's totally
urgent. I have to see him. He said he'd be here. Where
is he?"

"I don't have any idea," Len said.

"Well, I'm sure he'll be here soon. He promised me.
Can I wait for him inside?"

"Did you try out back?"

"Yes, of course," I said, trying to sound indignant, like
what do you think I am, a moron?

He sniffed the air like maybe he could smell deceit on
my breath. "Well, all right," he said. "What time was your
appointment, anyway?"

"Now. Maybe I'm a few minutes early . . . Thanks," I
said, pushing my way past him. He had given me an
opening and I took it. You have to be that way with
indecisive men. Assertive on the brink of bossy. They
love you for it—eventually. "I'll just wait in here for him,"
I said, making myself comfortable in his rather barren
living room. "If that's OK."

Len shrugged and left me alone. I heard him on the

stairs and then I heard sound in the water pipes. He was in the shower.

So Len the Celibate was one of Harvey Siegel's strays. No wonder Tom hadn't wanted to stick around too long.

I couldn't stick around long either. I had to get busy. I checked out the downstairs rooms, most of them pretty empty of stuff, until I found what had to be Harvey's study. This room was filled: desk, bookcases, leather couch, stereo and CDs, photographs and art work on every inch of wall space, a total clutter of books and papers.

Mission Impossible.

But I gave it a cursory search anyway. Looked on his desk and in his drawers . . . for what, I wasn't sure. Looked at his datebook. No entry for last Monday night: Kill Billy Blake.

What was I looking for anyway?

And if he had Lamont's stuff, would he keep it down here?

Riskier business, creeping up the stairs to the bedrooms.

Anyway I heard footsteps upstairs. Len took unnervingly short showers.

He came down and I was still primly sitting on one of the leather chairs in the otherwise empty-of-life living room.

"I have to go out now," he said. "I can't let you stay here unsupervised. Harvey doesn't allow clients in the house anyway as a usual thing. You'll have to go."

Courtesy was not Len's strong suit.

"Sure," I said. "I understand. He's not coming, is he? He's just abandoning me, like everyone else."

Len looked momentarily wounded. He sat down on the chair across from me. He was quite badly dressed in baggy jeans that weren't designed to be baggy jeans, just fit poorly, and a blue Oxford shirt with frayed sleeves, and he hadn't really done anything with his hair, like comb it, and he had an extremely ugly watch on a tight accordion band too far up on his arm. His shoes were brown leather with laces, and badly scuffed. He was overweight and paunchy and his skin was so white I would swear he hadn't been out in the sun for any extended period of time in several years.

"I wonder," he said, "if you've considered opening your heart to Jesus."

I almost fell over.

"No," I said, "I have to say I haven't. I go to therapy."

"Jesus will never abandon you," he said. "Think of it that way."

"I suppose that's true," I said.

"Yes. 'Though my father and mother forsake me, yet the Lord will receive me.' Sometimes we must abandon ourselves to a Higher Power. And trust that we are forgiven. Trust that we are saved. I can say with all humility that I am saved. I am forgiven. Even though I walk through the shadow of the valley of Death . . . And look around. This is the valley of Death. Look at how the Lord repays those who have sinned against him. 'Unless they be converted, God will sharpen his sword; he will bend and aim his bow, prepare his deadly weapons against them, and use fiery darts for arrows . . .' The Psalmist says of the wicked that their throats are open graves. Do you know what that means? I do. I have been inside those graves, the terrible horror of those graves. No more. Never again. I am washed in the blood of the Lamb."

I was getting very ready to leave. I stood up and said, "You need to go. I'm keeping you. I'm sorry."

"Do you know what the Lord wants from us? From

some of us? Vengeance is mine, says the Lord. 'Unjust witnesses have risen up; things I knew not of, they lay to my charge.' Scandal. They are so evil, so wicked. They are so evil, only those shielded and armored in the power of the Lord can dare face them."

"I'm sure that's true," I said, making my way to the front door, away from this lunatic. "Thanks so much. 'Bye." And I pushed the door open and escaped.

He did leave about ten minutes later, after making a phone call. I was across the street watching him through my telephoto lens.

As soon as he disappeared down the block in his big baggy jeans and leather jacket, I crept back up the side of the house and let myself in with the side door key which I had cleverly lifted from a hook in the kitchen.

The first thing I did was press re-dial to find out who he had called. I got an answering machine. You have reached... I copied the number down on my arm, for future reference, and headed upstairs.

Tom said he had left his bag here. Here, in this house. I had to find something here. If not here, where? This was the only place evidence could be, unless Evan lucked out with the army. Somehow lucking out with the army seemed like an oxymoron, on par with military intelligence.

The first door I opened at the top of the stairs was a guest room, clearly unoccupied. Maybe this was the room Tom had stayed in. Maybe, but probably not. I checked the closet for a Polo bag. Just weights and a pretty massive collection of porn. Not even very kinky porn, from what I saw of it.

The second was the master bedroom, Harvey's. A huge king size bed, a dresser, computer desk, wardrobe. It wasn't a very interesting room either except for the huge windows and the massive view across the valley—of Death, I guess Len would call it—toward Twin Peaks and Diamond Heights. With that out your window, who needed decoration?

I looked in his closet. He had an inordinate amount of running shoes, but no Polo bag to put them in.

But on his dresser, next to a framed photo of two very attractive young men, one of whom may or may not have been himself in his youth, there was a book of the poems of William Blake. It was too extraordinary and compelling a coincidence. I picked up the book . . . it had a picture of some Jehovah-looking character on the front . . . and opened up to the table of contents.

The table of contents was almost unreadable. Scawled across the page in black magic marker was Tom's tag: BLISS.

His book.

OK. Onward. I stuffed the book in my bag and went to the next room.

The door was locked.

I felt above the doorjamb and retrieved the key.

If this was Len's room, he sure wasn't too bright.

I unlocked the door and opened it.

It was Len's room. It had to be.

It was a small room, dark. The drapes were closed, thick drapes that kept out all the light. Hanging over the bed, a twin bed, Spartan looking, was a red lamp, the sort you see in churches, sanctuary lamps, they're called, that indicate the presence on the altar of consecrated hosts.

This Catholic stuff was all coming back to me.

There was a huge crucifix over the bed, painted in full color, practically life-size, Jesus hanging on the cross in agony, blood pouring from his wounds. Where on earth did he find something like this? On the opposite wall was a reproduction of the Martyrdom of St. Sebastian, the handsome young man tied to a tree writhing in pain, a hundred arrows sticking into his flesh.

Beneath this painting was a table with dozens of candles on it. I could see the room at night, candles burning before Sebastian's body, the red lamp lit as well, Len the Celibate flagellating himself with a whip he bought on Castro Street, down in that valley of death, in an S and M joint.

I didn't want to look in his closets. In fact, all I wanted was to get out of there fast.

I turned back to the door. In the corner next to it was a small table. The table was covered with flowers, not in a vase but just lying in various stages of decay on the wood. In the center of the table was a picture in a frame, a black and white photograph. I went up to the table and picked up the picture.

It was the most striking image I had ever seen of a black Christ. Suspended from two posts as though on a cross, face masked, body covered with lines like wounds, like cuts, though maybe they were tendrils of vines, and maybe his belly was slit open, or maybe those were vines too, spilling out of him. In black and white and slightly unfocused, you couldn't tell what was plant and what was his own body. He had become that image: a god-man turning into earth, into flower.

My throat was so dry I could barely swallow.

I had found Tom's photograph of Lamont.

CHAPTER 25

I drove home with a bag full of things I had ripped off from Harvey Siegel's house: a book of William Blake's poetry, a photograph of Lamont Bliss's death, a side door key in case I ever needed to go back, and Len's telephone book, just to see who he knew.

I didn't really think he'd know somebody named Randy Dunbar. But miracles happen. Or so I'm told.

It'd have to be a miracle, though.

Because all I knew for sure was that Len had a photograph that must have come from Lamont's camera. It didn't necessarily mean he'd ever had the camera in his possession, or that he even knew who it was a picture of. Someone could have given him the photograph, seeing how he was so into sado-masochistic iconography. That he had it didn't prove anything, didn't even implicate him in anything, unless he was artistic consultant for the murder of Billy Blake.

I could of course try to figure out who had done the enlargement. A commercial lab would stamp the back of the photo. Maybe I could go there and try to find out who had brought the negative in, or if they had processed the roll.

Actually you'd think a lab might report something like this.

In Lyman Jasper country, yeah. But here in the valley of Death, it was highly unlikely.

I had come up with a lot of nothing. Evan would wind up pulling the whole thing together, finding Lieutenant Randy Dunbar, United States Army, saving the day, as usual, by the most direct and simple route. As for me, I now had a moral obligation to call Elizabeth and then, before I drove anywhere, I absolutely had to go to sleep.

"Oh my God, Alexandra!" my sister screeched right into my ear, "you know a murderer!"

"Elizabeth, this is America, remember? Innocent until proven guilty? Remember?"

"Oh, yes. That's all well and good in junior high civics, but in reality, Alex, the police do not arrest the *wrong* man. They just don't. If he was arrested, he's 99.9 per cent sure of being convicted. That's a fact."

"Look, Elizabeth, I can't argue with you about this. He's my friend. I love him. He's innocent. I have to get him out if I can. Would you please lend me some money?"

"Doesn't he have parents? A family? Why do you have to bail him out?"

"Because his family's in Oregon. And they're not rich people, Elizabeth. And I am family, or almost. You are too. I'm going to marry him."

I could hear my sister sit down hard on the closest available surface.

"You're marrying a murderer?"

"No, actually I'm marrying a serial killer. That makes sense, doesn't it? I'm just the wacky sort of person to do something like that, aren't I? Get a fucking life, Elizabeth! I'm telling you, he didn't kill this man. It's a mistake."

"They all say that."

"Sometimes they're right. This time I'm right. Evan believes him too. Evan's a friend of his. Do you want me to ask Evan to call you when he gets home? He will."

"I'll have to discuss it with Jeremy."

"Of course."

"Jeremy is very much against gay rights and all that, you understand? This man isn't gay, is he?"

"No, Elizabeth. In fact, listen, if Jeremy really disapproves of the gay lifestyle, you can tell him that the man Sean is accused of killing was a very prominent member of the gay community. And African-American on top of it! Jeremy might be really happy to bail out a man who allegedly managed to rid the world of a black and a gay man at the same time."

"You are impossible!" my sister said, but I thought I detected a little glimmer of amusement in her voice. "He's not that bad."

"Lyman Jasper, Elizabeth? No offense or anything, but can you get worse?"

"Well, you'll be happy to know that Jeremy and I are not attending that fundraiser after all."

"No? Don't tell me Jeremy's seen the light and joined the Libertarians!"

"No, listen. Jeremy is not as bad as you like to think. He has principles. Turns out that the American Values Foundation, though it's a very legal, above-board organization and everything, gives an enormous amount of money to this radical, militant, fundamentalist group called the Army of God. And not even Jeremy would associate himself with . . ."

"What's it called again?" I asked her. "The army of . . ."

I didn't have to move. I knew somebody was standing right behind me. I could see his shadow falling on the kitchen floor. I knew he'd come in through the window behind me, the window I had stupidly opened. I knew he was going to grab me around the throat and strangle me, in one second I'd be dead, one second wasn't long enough to say anything worth saying to Elizabeth, like help, not even help . . .but

"Help! Help!" I yelled into the phone and then I swung around with the receiver aloft in my hand ready to have my last act in this life be bashing this fucker's head in with my cordless phone . . .

He grabbed my wrist and held it so I couldn't move. I could hear my sister's voice yelling my name through the receiver for the one second it took Charlie Coyote, now dressed in army fatigues, to twist the receiver out of my hand and switch the OFF button off.

"OK," he said, "You know why I'm here, right? I have to have it, Alice. Where is it?"

"I don't have it," I said. "I don't know where Sean put it. But it's not here."

"I don't want to hurt anybody," he said.

I laughed at him. Nervous laughter. Terrified laughter. I thought he must think I was a complete moron or something. And yet he had let go of my wrist and I was free, more or less. For the moment. Free but a little too scared to move. And naturally there wasn't any sharp instrument handy. Evan was too neat a housekeeper to leave sharp instruments lying around.

"I never thought it was you," I said.

"You have no idea how important this is. Now sit down. I guess I'm just going to have to look for it myself."

I remembered my hands were still free. I pushed him back toward the window as hard as I could and made a dash for the door. He caught me there and grabbed me. I kicked him but he turned me around and pinned me against the door with his body up against mine so I couldn't maneuver.

"I told you I don't want to hurt you. Why don't you just fucking sit down!"

"You don't want to hurt me? Who the fuck do you think you're kidding? Just tell me this, *Charlie*. What fucking general are you people killing everybody to protect? And how did they let a faggot like you in the army anyway? Or is this what they do with gays in the military? Turn them into fucking assassins and spies!"

"Man, Alice, are you ever out of control! The only army I'm in is the Queer Nation army. You got to be 4-F to get in."

He let go of me and backed away.

"You want to go out the door, go. I'm not gonna stop you."

"Who are you then?"

"Charlie Coyote. We met already. Remember?"

"You're a friend of Brendan's. Of Tom's."

"Of Brendan's, yeah. Tom . . . the head-banger? Don't know him that well."

"He spent a night at your place last week."

"Yeah. So?"

"He left a camera there."

"No. He didn't leave anything. Tagged the fucking building, that's all he did. Like a fucking adolescent."

"And you're really here for the interview? What do you want it for?"

"What for? Names, Alice. Names. Lots of names."

"So you can out them?"

"That's right. So we can out the fuckers. See what happens when the biggest homophobes in America turn out to be homos themselves. I'd like to see that, wouldn't you? How they deal with a little contradiction and hypocrisy. I think it'd be quite a show."

I agreed it would be really cool, but that I still didn't have the interview, that Sean would never leave it here because people were getting killed for it, in case he hadn't heard. That the thing to do was to go visit Sean in the lock-up and ask him where the fucking thing was. Just ask him. Don't rip my house apart.

Charlie, for all his macho army clothes, was also pretty easy to boss around. He agreed to talk to Sean and left—by the door.

I locked everything behind him and pulled Len's phone book out of my bag.

It wasn't the United States Army at all. It was the Army of God.

I looked in Len's phone book under A for Army. I

looked under D for Dunbar and R for Randy. Nothing. Then I dialed the number that Len had called just before he left, the number I had copied down on my hand. Probably his mother.

A woman answered. "Americans For Family Values, can I help you?"

"Is Mr. Dunbar there?"

"Just a moment," she said. There were a lot of clicks and beeps on the line. Then a man's voice almost blasted my ear drum out, "Who's calling?"

"I'm trying to reach Mr. Dunbar."

"Who are you?"

"I'm sorry," I said. "I can only speak to Mr. Dunbar."

"Well, you have the wrong number. He doesn't work out of this office. You'll have to try the Foundation."

"Thanks," I said and managed to switch the phone off before I gave a victory yelp.

The line went from Len to someone at Americans for Family Values to Dunbar at the Foundation to the cadre of the Army of God. From mild, meek Len the Celibate to those brutes in black. A direct line.

I'd done it. I'd made the connection. I was happy. I was also so tired I couldn't keep my eyes open another minute. Half an hour of sleep and I'd be fine. I set my alarm and crawled under the covers.

But I couldn't sleep. I had that feeling you get just before an earthquake, that really hysterical energy, that absolute wakefulness.

I was in the grip of paranoia. I thought someone was on the roof. Then I thought I heard someone outside my window. Then at the back door.

Someone was at the back door.

I got out of bed and went into the kitchen. I wanted that little pistol from the Mercedes, I wanted to stand back from them and shoot them and not have to get dirty doing it. But we didn't have a gun in the house. The best I could do was pick up a butcher knife and crawl behind the couch, where at least I could see which way they were coming, and wait.

They came in through the rear door. Broke the glass without making a sound. I sure didn't hear them. All of a sudden, there they were in the hall, two of them in basic black. They had stockings pulled down over their faces and latex gloves over their hands. They were scary as hell.

One went into my bedroom, one crept along the hall right toward me.

I could hear my heart beating, so I assumed he could hear it as well and was following the sound. He looked in Evan's room. He crossed the hall and looked into Jake's. Checking for warm bodies. He came into the living room and looked around.

I wondered if I could jump out at him like Anthony Perkins in *Psycho* and stab him in the heart.

He was coming right toward the couch.

He was so close I could see a run in the stocking over his face.

I crouched lower and tried very hard not to breathe.

He took one more step. The floorboard creaked.

The silence afterwards was profound, as though the whole house were holding its breath like I was.

Then the earthquake hit.

Everything began shaking, the whole building, the floor under my feet. There was a tremendous rushing-moving-crashing sound, glass shattering, wood splintering, feet pounding, all in full stereo, and male voices yelling, and bodies falling, and I just curled up in a ball, put my arms around my head, one hand still clutching the knife, and waited for Armageddon to end.

It lasted a few minutes. When it sounded over, I eased myself slowly and carefully into the scene, rising up from behind the couch, butcher knife still firmly in my hand, to find two dozen men in full combat gear squeezed into the living room, some poking around the kitchen, some poking around the hall, the two intruders on the floor, handcuffed, guns pointed at their heads, somebody barking orders, or maybe it was the Miranda warnings, or maybe they were asking where they'd stashed my body . . . And, *voilà!*, there I was, momentarily invisible again, until I cleared my throat and found all gun barrels suddenly pointing in my direction.

Thankfully when the SWAT team breaks down your doors they yell POLICE! so you know exactly who it is who's stopped by for tea.

I had managed to sit down on the couch and was lighting a cigarette, still shaking and struggling to stay cool, surrounded by heavily armed men in bullet-proof vests, when my sister marched in, wearing a Christian Dior suit under an Yves Saint Laurent overcoat and smelling intoxicatingly of Gio. Elizabeth, it appeared, had heard my cry for help over the telephone and come over from Mill Valley in her red Jag to rescue me, dressed to the nines and bringing the entire San Francisco police force with her.

CHAPTER 26

My house looked like a war zone, some police officer dressed like a ninja was asking me if I could please answer a million questions and my sister's Jaguar was double parked outside. It was a nightmare.

I got so tangled up in trying to answer the cop's questions that I finally told him this was all connected to Billy Blake's murder and that I really had to talk to Detective Kagehiro about it.

I guess it was my soul speaking. The soul can only take so much complexity, so much elaboration. Then it goes simple on you.

The simple truth. Maybe, finally, we actually had it.

It was a real group thing at Kagehiro's desk. I was there in my usual rags and tatters as Elizabeth so candidly put it ("God, can't you even dress well for the *police*!"). By contrast, Elizabeth was as well dressed as you can be without holding a royal title. Paul the lawyer was in his lawyer suit. Evan wore his San Francisco Pollution Control jacket. Jake showed up as we were leaving the house in his waiter clothes and came along for the ride, posing as another member of the extended family.

I was acutely aware of Sean's absence.

Then there was the police contingent. Kagehiro, looking dryer than last time I'd seen him. Another plainclothes detective, African-American. A Latina stenographer. We were an entire rainbow coalition right there.

Paul had told me that Sean hadn't given a statement to the police since his arrest the night before. They had had one conference that morning and Paul had agreed to represent him. A bail hearing was set for the following day.

So it was up to me.

I told practically the whole story as I knew it, from the beginning to the end. I had worked it out in my head so it made sense even with certain elisions. I told them that Sean had realized right off that there was a connection between Jeff Taylor's death and Billy Blake's. The connection was the interview. I told them how we had found Billy Blake and gone to speak to him the night he was killed. I told them about how we had been attacked by the men in black the night before, how Sean had been kidnapped, even how I had shot them and what they had told us in the alley. I produced the photograph of Lamont that I had found in Len's room. I said I didn't know how he got it, which was true, more or less. I said I didn't know who had killed Lamont. I didn't mention Tom at all.

"Why didn't you tell us all this last night?" Kagehiro asked me. He was trying to sound avuncular, but I detected annoyance in his voice.

Paul answered for me. He said that I had quite reasonably wanted to speak to my attorney first.

"I would like to know the status of my clients at this point," Paul added. I guess I was his client now too.

"We aren't charging the young lady with anything," Kagehiro said. "Until someone appears to make a complaint with a bullet in his balls. As for your other client, I don't see what these two men we arrested today have to do with him. Right now all we can hold them on is burglary. We will certainly inquire about any connection they may have to the deaths of Taylor and Blake, but as far as Lamont Bliss is concerned, there's nothing to connect these men with that murder."

He was right of course; there was nothing. And unless

one of the Army of God men confessed outright, there probably wasn't any way to convict them of killing Jeff and Billy either. They were professional, they didn't leave prints. What did we have against them anyway? A confidential interview, all hearsay now that both interviewer and interviewee were dead, that allegedly implicated their boss in homosexual practices, him among many others—totally circumstantial. A photograph of a dead man found in somebody else's bedroom—irrelevant. A kidnapping that involved a murder suspect and his girlfriend—highly questionable. A confession that they were in the pay of a lieutenant in the Army of God—Paul had already told me that everything they'd said to us would get blown out of the water at a trial. We were holding guns to their heads, after all.

"But he's innocent," I said. Tom's name was at the tip of my tongue. I felt like it was strangling me. But Tom who? I didn't even know his last name.

It wasn't up to me. Sean had given his word. It was his life on the line, his call. Maybe he thought, maybe he and Paul together thought, he could get off without implicating Tom. Maybe there wasn't enough evidence. Maybe it wasn't necessary to drag Tom into this.

A uniformed cop approached Kagehiro and slipped a piece of paper onto his desk. I was watching him so closely, I could see him take in the words, squeeze meaning out of them. He looked up, over the table, past me, to some focal spot at the far end of the room.

"Do you know a man named Oliver Jefferson Powell?"

I swivelled around in my chair so I could see what Kagehiro was looking at across the room. He was standing between two uniformed policemen in his grunge clothes, his wrists handcuffed in front of him, skinny and sallow and poor, but as soon as he saw me, he smiled.

"He's just turned himself in for the murder of Lamont Bliss."

Oliver Jefferson Powell.

Tom.

They let Sean out of the lock-up and we hugged and kissed and danced in the street and went off, *en famille*, and in a red Jag, for beers, vegeburgers and smokes. All of us but Paul, who had just taken on a new client.

"Now if Len the Celibate would only have a religious crisis and go talk to Kagehiro," I said. "He could blow those God people right out of the water."

"I'll go talk to him," Evan said. "I'll get Chris to go with me. Chris can work the program. He used to have a lover who was into twelve steps to God, or some such thing. He knows the ropes."

"They like getting tied up," I said. "Ropes work."

We were all happy. We were all victorious. We laughed hard and drank hard. Except for Sean, who seemed distant, withdrawn, almost sad. Evan noticed it too, and being Evan, just asked.

"Hey, Sean, what's up, man? You really tired? Time to go home?"

I liked the way he said home, meaning our home.

"No, I'm cool," he said. But he only stayed with us for about five minutes before he spaced out again.

"We're going to have to clean up when we get home, you know," Jake the Practical said. "Clean up all that broken glass and secure the doors in the house. The cops only do the busting. They don't send in the cleaners. Citizens have to clean up after them as a contribution to public health and safety."

"Let's just go to sleep and call the landlord in the morning," Evan said. "I'm wasted."

He had spent hours trying to locate Lieutenant Randy Dunbar of the U.S. Army. Poor Evan.

We all piled back into the Jaguar and went home. Our house was still standing. Nobody had come in and robbed us in our absence. The Army of God was under lock and key and the Castro was safe again.

"Jeff's memorial service is tomorrow night," Sean said to me as I was lying in his arms on the verge of sleep.

"We should go, huh?"

"I'd like to," he said. "Would you come with me?"

"Sure," I said. "You don't have to ask."

"I don't?"

"Well, not about that."

"What do I have to ask about?"

"Oh, you know. Ordering sushi for two at restaurants, renting Bergman videos, getting a cock ring."

"I was thinking about a cock ring."

"Oh Jesus."

He squeezed me. "Not!" he said.

I tried to squeeze him back but before the thought got from my brain to my arms, I was asleep.

CHAPTER 27

I woke up the next day and realized it was Thursday morning. I had to be living in a time warp or a Gertrude Stein novel. A continuous present, says Stein, is a continuous present. The soul lives atemporally. OK, fine, but how could all *this* have happened in a single week, from Thursday to Thursday, *Star Trek* night to *Star Trek* night?

The enumerator comes knocking and nothing is ever the same again: sex isn't the same, poetry, what you think of justice, honor—it all gets turned around. Even time isn't the same.

It was Thursday again, according to the morning paper. Clinton had been president a week and a day and the ban on gays in the military hadn't been lifted. Big surprise. The military was just saying no. The American Values Foundation was saying no, too, and saying it right in San Francisco, where they were all gathering to hear Lyman Jasper denounce the anti-American homosexual conspiracy and collect big bucks at his fundraiser Friday night.

But Thursday for us meant going to Jeff's memorial service, Jeff who had been alive a week ago, ringing doorbells on Liberty Street. I'd never even met him. I missed him. I had missed his whole life. I'd never met him and I never would.

I sat over the morning paper and felt angry about everything. Angry and sad. I was sad for everyone: Lamont, Jeff, Billy, Tom. Even Len the Celibate, the deluded, who if he had a car might put on his bumper one of those stickers that says Jesus is My Best Friend. It made Choose Death seem incredibly brave and sane.

I thought of Fuller too. Charlie Coyote. Brendan Maddox. All of them.

I was sad and mad, pissed off and on the verge of tears. I knew in my heart the men who murdered Jeff, who slaughtered Billy Blake, those horrible men with stockings over their heads and latex gloves over their hands, would never, never get what they deserved. And the men who sent them—Randy Dunbar, Lyman Jasper— wouldn't lose a night's sleep over any of it.

Sean was up and dressed before I'd had my second cup

of coffee, that is, before I was awake. He collected all his enumeration folders and interviews and his bag of blood samples, and announced that he was going to the University to turn them in and resign, if he wasn't fired already.

"I don't think Lydia will be too pleased that I spent a night in jail for killing a member of one of our sample households," he said. "Anyway, I can't do this job anymore."

"You're turning in the interview?" I asked.

"What interview?"

"Billy's, of course. *The* interview."

"Oh," he said. "*That* interview. 'The road of excess leads to the palace of wisdom.' William Blake."

"Is that a yes or a no?"

"That's a proverb of hell," he said, and kissed me. "I'll be back later. You'll be here?"

"Sure," I said. "I live here."

After he left I wandered around the house, looking for traces of him. There was nothing of him left anywhere. He had gone and taken everything with him.

I spent the afternoon looking through the want ads, listening to sad music and wondering if I'd ever see Sean again. I kept telling myself that of course he'd be back, why wouldn't he? But then I'd think, what if everything that had happened between us was wrapped up in what had happened to Jeff? And that now that that quest was over, we'd just part as easily as we had met? What would I do if Sean just disappeared from my life as accidentally as he had appeared in it?

If it happens, it happens, I said to myself. Just get over it.

But at five minutes after 5, Sean arrived at the door

bearing a six-pack of Red Tail ale and a bunch of enormous sunflowers.

"Kiss me," he said. "I'm broke, starved for affection and unemployed."

I put on a black dress for Jeff.

Sean checked me out in the mirror, went right to my closet, dug around for awhile and emerged with a Portuguese scarf, black with big red flowers on it.

"You need some color," he said. "You're too beautiful to wear black."

He was wearing black too—black shirt, black jeans, black leather motorcycle jacket—with a red bandana around his neck.

Evan and Jake were home by then, too, and said they were coming along. Funeral services, *en famille*.

The service was being held in the gay community's church, a few blocks from our house.

We were early or something, because there weren't many people there. We sat in the third row, in case nobody else came. It was heartbreaking, the thought that no one else might come.

But at a quarter of the hour, like a trampling herd, everybody arrived, en masse. There must have been some dinner or something first, some pre-service event. It was as though all of Queer Nation in army boots was occupying the church. Angry men, sorrowful men. Sean stood up and hugged one of them, pale, lanky, wearing a workshirt with a black tie, who looked like he had been crying a lot and who I guessed was Brendan Maddox. Charlie Coyote was there and he came over and gave Sean a hug, too, which I thought unusual and somewhat endearing. I caught a glimpse of Len the Celibate hovering around the back of the church. By then it was standing room only. The only person I missed seeing was Tom.

It started with everybody singing "Tears in Heaven."

"Oh, *Brendan*," Sean groaned, looking at the program we'd been handed as we came in. "Whose fucking funeral service is this anyway? He should have let me do the music."

"What would you have picked?" I asked, thinking of Pantera's hard core metal chords blasting the glass right out of the windows.

"Start with a recording of Dylan Thomas reciting 'And Death Shall Have No Dominion.' Instead of the preacher, play the 'Deploration on the Death of Ockeghem' by Josquin Desprez. After everybody says what a great guy he was, Marianne Faithfull singing 'Working Class Hero.' From denial to grief to rage—that's the trajectory I'd aim for. But Brendan's such a . . ."

"Sshh," I said. Brendan was crying in the first pew. "I don't think the music's that important right now."

"Yeah," Sean said, following my glance. "I guess it finally hit him."

It was hitting me too, and I didn't even know Jeff.

The minister said a few words, and then, one by one, friends of Jeff's stood in front of the congregation and talked about him or recited his favorite poems or his favorite one-liners. They talked about his warmth, his sense of humor, how easy it was to be with him, and some of them cried outright and talked about how he had seen them through horrible times, how just knowing he was there was the most important thing, that he would always be there, someone you could rely on, someone who would never let you down.

How terribly he would be missed.

It was over. The minister began moving toward the podium. There was no one else waiting to speak.

Except Sean. He let go of my hand, got up and walked to the front of the church.

He introduced himself and said he had been a friend of Jeff's. Then it seemed he lost his voice or his train of thought. He stared at Brendan for a few long seconds. He shifted his gaze and looked at me. Charlie, sitting in the row in front of me, just to my right, broke into a grin, a really big, stupid grin. Sean took a deep breath.

"I wasn't Jeff's lover," he said. "But I loved him. And I guess he loved me too, because he entrusted me with something before he died. It was an interview for the AIDS study he worked for." He opened his jacket and pulled a long booklet out of his inside pocket. He unfolded the booklet and held it up so everyone could see it. "It was this interview . . ."

I sat still as stone. I was still breathing but it felt as though I had left my body and was floating above it. He was going to do it. Charlie knew, that's why he was smiling like that. But no one else knew, not really, and so there was that collective puzzlement, that squirmy sort of wondering. Something's not going according to form. What's happening here?

He paused. Somebody was tramping up the side aisle toward the front of the church. It was Fuller, dressed like a Queer Nation commando and looking nasty, half-dragging, half-escorting a totally terrified Len the Celibate to the front row.

"Let's hear it," Fuller said to Sean, to everybody, and pushed Len into a seat. "Into the mic, man! Into the mic!"

Now the church was so still you could hear a child talking to someone out on the street, you could hear a blast of music from a passing car radio, but you couldn't hear a single man inside the church take a breath of air.

Sean spoke into the mic. I closed my eyes and just listened to the beautiful sound of my lover's voice telling 200 gay men that their friend, Jeff Taylor, had been murdered to protect the reputation of the leader of the American Values Foundation.

Then he struck the *coup de grâce*.

He outed Lyman Jasper.

They mobbed him in the aisle. Like he was a quarterback who had just thrown the final pass, fifty yards, sixty maybe. Won the game in the final seconds. The Hail Mary pass. They mobbed him like that.

Someone started singing "Amazing Grace."

Louder voices started chanting something else, more militant, filled with rage.

It was like that, all the time. Grace on the one hand, rage on the other.

It was what we were living in.

It's where we were.

Are.

As we left the church, he passed something to Charlie Coyote.

"Your ball," he said.

Justice is not something you get. It's something you make. Like love. You make it. We did. Do.

We walked home with our arms around each other. The moon was out and the stars.

"Well, this should sure put a damper on old Lyman's fundraiser tomorrow night," Sean said.

"I'd like to see him locked up for life in Pelican Bay. I'd like him to have the whole damn prison to himself."

He stopped in front of our house and stared up at the midnight blue sky and the twinkling stars.

"I hope it's what he wanted," Sean said. "I hope wherever he is, he's just a little bit pleased."

CHAPTER 28

The road of excess, Sean told me, quoting William Blake, leads to the palace of wisdom.

Sometime during the night, I arrived at that palace.

I had been stupid. I had thought he was going to leave me. I had thought he was going to be like the others. It was my fate, I thought, to be abandoned by men.

That night I understood that I was wrong. This one was different. I became wise at last.

"Is this real, Alex?" he asked me at one point. "Because, you know, I always thought it was, but I wasn't sure until now."

He said, "You told me you'd trust me and you did. I had to lie to you over and over and even when you knew I was lying to you, you never doubted me. You stuck it out all the way."

He said, "I've never loved anyone the way I love you."

He said, "I can't believe this is happening."

"What?" I asked him, but I knew.

"Do you still want to marry me?"

"Ask," I said.

He did.

By the time we got up the next afternoon, blissful and unconscionably happy, all hell had broken loose.

Charlie Coyote had been quite thorough in contacting

the press. Queer Nation was outing Lyman Jasper with all the ammunition they had. And they had plenty of it.

Including Len the Celibate.

Charlie himself arrived at our house in person in the early afternoon to tell us what was up. He was a happy man. Not as happy as we were; we were out in space somewhere. Charlie was planted firmly on the ground, but happily planted. He had done it. Lyman Jasper was history.

"And," he said, "we have Leonard. Those fuckers are going down, Sean. He talked to Kagehiro this morning. All morning. I took him down personally, hand delivered him. Those fuckers are gonna bite it. Big time."

We drank Red Tail and listened to what Len the Celibate had told Kagehiro. What a story it was.

Len had been the spy in the house of love, or in this case, at Queer Nation meetings. He had been searching for salvation for some time before he ran into Randy Dunbar at some revival meeting. Dunbar knew a gift from God when he saw it, and here one was: a tortured homosexual who wanted to find Jesus and be born again and was willing to do anything to join the saved. Dunbar told him AIDS was the way God was punishing homosexuals for their sins. He told him he could be saved from that fate if he accepted Jesus into his life, and that in exchange for divine forgiveness and love, he would have to hang out with queers in the Castro and make reports to Dunbar about what was happening in that Valley of Death and those dens of iniquity. There was a war going on between good and evil; the Army of God needed to have its agents out in the field, living with the sinners but, through God's protection, being uncorrupted by them.

Len had heard rumors of the interview long before Robert Slatley came out. Brendan evidently couldn't keep quiet about this hot information his lover had on certain prominent homophobes. Len had dutifully reported it to Randy Dunbar, just like he reported everything else— when Queer Nation was holding demos and whether they were supporting a certain candidate or boycotting the state of Colorado, whatever. Then Slatley came out and the news must have resonated in the higher echelons of the American Values Foundation. In any case, Dunbar contacted Len and told him to find out who in Queer Nation had this information. It was no secret in the community. Brendan's lover was Jeff Taylor and he was working as an enumerator for the AIDS study. He had the information and the only place he could have gotten it was from the gay man Slatley—and, as it turned out— Jasper had been having sex with: Billy Blake. Eliminate Jeff and Billy, recover the interview, and nobody's the wiser.

"Fucking amazing," Sean said. "But how did you get him to tell you all this?"

"Didn't tell me any of it. He told Fuller."

"Fuller? Why?"

Charlie smiled demonically. "Fuller ... had certain means of persuasion," he said.

We both leaned a little closer across the table to Charlie.

"You don't want to know," he said. "Fuller's a maniac. Badly damaged. Out of control."

We still wanted to know.

Charlie wanted to tell us, too. He cracked open a beer and grinned at us.

"In a totally perverted way, it's totally beautiful."

After the service, Fuller and a buddy of his, another street hustler and like Fuller, rampantly HIV positive, had taken Len the Celibate, quite against his will, to the friend's apartment on 16th Street, the same one I had followed Fuller to Monday afternoon. They had stripped him naked and tied him to the bed and explained that they were the Army of Death, the AIDS squadron, and their assignment was to infect him with the virus though they intended to make the whole experience as pleasurable for him as possible.

Unless of course he was willing to tell them some things.

He told them everything.

"What about the photographs of Lamont?" I asked Charlie. "Did he say anything about them?"

"Sure he did. Len was a snoop. When he found Lamont's camera at Harvey's he took the film out and had it developed. Maybe he'd get pictures of naked boys. Maybe Lamont and Tom having sex. He got a little more than he bargained for though. Hot stuff on that roll. Of course he told Dunbar about it. Handed the photos over, except for one. He had to keep one for himself. To jerk off in front of.

"He told Fuller that he didn't know that Dunbar's people had murdered Jeff. He swore he didn't even get the connection when Billy was killed. He believed that whoever had killed Billy was the same person who had killed Lamont, that it was some gay ripper, certainly not the Christians doing it. Even when you outed Jasper, even then he thought it was a trick, that it was just the queers lying and being wicked as usual. What convinced him finally was Fuller's dick pointing at his ass."

"I'd have thought he'd love being a martyr," I said. "Dying for Jesus at the hands of evil homosexuals, the army of Satan."

"Not at their *hands*, Alice," Charlie chucked. "No, not exactly at their *hands*."

"He must have known though," Sean said. "He just

needed a slight religious crisis, like you said, Alex. To clear up the confusion."

"Fuller," I said. "The wrath of God."

"In person," Charlie said. "And the wrath of God always works, one way or the other." He offered his hand to Sean. "Listen, man. Thanks for everything." Then he held out his hand to me. "Alice, thanks a lot. And I'm real sorry about Wednesday."

"It's OK," I said.

He grinned at Sean. "So, see you around."

"Later," Sean said.

"Yeah," Charlie said, grinning at me now. "Breed well and prosper."

It was my turn to make dinner. In fact, I was in the hole for about five dinners; I'd be cooking for the next week. Sean and I went to the Safeway to shop and ran into about fifty people we knew. It took hours to pick up pasta and vegetables and beer. We couldn't decide between pesto or primavera, spaced out over the avocados, couldn't find the perfect head of lettuce. But by some miracle dinner was actually ready by the time Jake and Evan got home from work. It started raining again and the rain pattered on the windows while we watched the 7 o'clock *Star Trek* re-run, something I hadn't done all week. After *Star Trek* was over, we sat around the kitchen drinking beer. Sean and I divied up the want ads. Jake and Evan picked up that conversation we'd been having the week before on the nature of the soul.

"How's this for a working definition?" Evan asked, opening the book he'd been reading by Thomas Moore called *Care of the Soul*. "The soul is the infinite depth in a person or of a society comprising all the mysterious aspects that go together to make up our identity."

"Infinite depth," Sean said. "I like that in a soul."

"Mysterious aspects," I said. "I like that in a soul, too."

"And he got 'identity' in there," Jake added. "Very postmodern of him."

"You guys," Evan sighed. "You're impossible."

"It works, Evan," Sean said, grinning at him. "Really. Infinite depths, mysterious aspects and identity. He covered the bases. Let's drink to the soul, infinite and mysterious."

We spent the evening like that, sitting around the table, happy together, drinking, talking, listening to the rain.

Night. We had collected all the candles in the house and lit them in my room, turning it into a magical place of light and shadow. Now and then the rain pattered against the window, now and then we heard voices from the street. We made love, we talked. It was just where we wanted to be, after all, in our own space, in love and in rapture, but also still in the world, the street still calling to us, the city waiting for us, along with all the tasks we had to do in the morning when we woke up. For one thing, we still had to get Tom out of jail.

"You know, Alex," Sean said, staring up at the dancing shapes on the ceiling, "I really like your brother. Evan's a cool guy. No, that's not right. He's cool, yeah. He's also a good man."

"You're a good man, too," I said. "You were willing to take the rap for Tom. You protected him. Why did you do that?"

He didn't say anything for awhile. The candles flickered. I felt him breathing against me. I thought maybe he had fallen asleep. Then he said, "See, Alex, I could have been him. I was headed down that road when I was fifteen, sixteen. All it takes is a couple of lousy breaks. Get kicked out of your house, hustle for money, get HIV, do some bad drugs, hit somebody too hard. I was just lucky. Just lucky, that's all. But I figured, if it had been different, if my life had turned out like his, I'd want somebody to take care of me. Just once."

"He came through for you, too, didn't he?"

"He sure did."

"Did you give him that copy of Blake's poems?"

"Did he have a copy of Blake's poems? No, I didn't give it to him."

I dug around in my bag and found Tom's book of Blake's poetry, the table of contents tagged with Lamont's name, BLISS, and handed it to Sean.

"Fuck me," he said. He flipped through it until he came to a page that had a few stanzas boxed in red marker with stars all around it. "I guess he liked this passage."

"Read it to me."

"I love these lines, too," he said. "They're like a prophecy of our time. Self-satisfied, self-righteous, religious men rejoicing in the pain and sufferings of others. And the poet saying, I refuse. I will not rejoice."

"Please read," I said.

He pulled a candle closer to the bed and squinted at the page.

"What is the price of Experience?" he began. *"Do men buy it for a song?*
Or wisdom for a dance in the street? No, it is bought with the price
Of all a man hath, his house, his wife, his children.
Wisdom is sold in the desolate market where none come to buy,
And in the wither'd field where the farmer plows for bread in vain.

It is an easy thing to triumph in the summer's sun

*And in the vintage & to sing on the waggon loaded
    with corn.*
It is an easy thing to talk of patience to the afflicted,
*To speak the laws of prudence to the houseless
    wanderer,*
To listen to the hungry raven's cry in wintry season
*When the red blood is fill'd with wine & with the
    marrow of lambs.*

It is an easy thing to laugh at wrathful elements,
*To hear the dog howl at the wintry door, the ox in
    the slaughter house moan;*
*To see a god on every wind & a blessing on every
    blast;*
*To hear sounds of love in the thunder storm that
    destroys our enemies' house;*
*To rejoice in the blight that covers his field, & the
    sickness that cuts off his children,*
*While our olive & vine sing & laugh round our
    door, & our children bring fruits and flowers.*

*Then the groan & the dolor are quite forgotten, & the
    slave grinding at the mill,*
*And the captive in chains, & the poor in the
    prison, & the soldier in the field*
*When the shatter'd bone hath laid him groaning
    among the happier dead.*

*It is an easy thing to rejoice in the tents of
    prosperity:*
Thus could I sing & thus rejoice: but it is not so with
    me."

He snapped the book shut, and the candle nearest to it
went out.

Yes, I thought, it was an easy thing to see God's hand in the blight that covers another man's field and the sickness that cuts off his children. And it was easy to forget the captive in chains and the poor in prison and the dying in the hospice. Except for people like Evan and Jeff Taylor and Sean, who didn't forget.

"I hope we don't have to take this literally," I said. "I want to rejoice for a while."

"Oh, we can rejoice," he said. "Just not in the tents of prosperity."

"You mean, as long as we're unemployed?"

"As long as you want, Alex," he said.

The wind blew hard on the windows. We put out all the candles, curled up together and fell asleep listening to the rain.